The Addict's Web

The Addict's Web

A Novel About

Trauma, Drugs & Recovery

Diana Wolfson

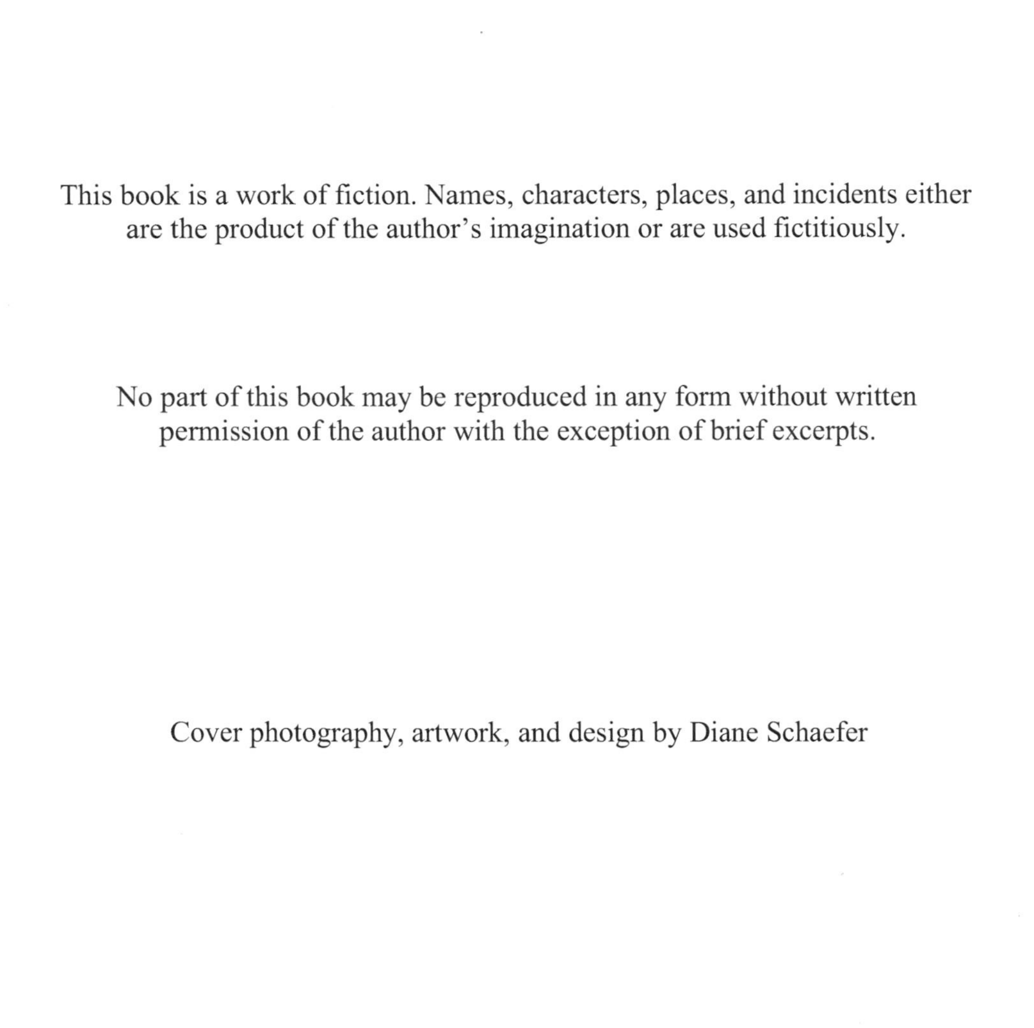

Cover photography, artwork, and design by Diane Schaefer

ISBN-9798670873239

Dedication

To those who struggle with addiction
and
to those who struggle along with them.

NOTES TO THE READER

The Addict's Web is a work of fiction based on a true story.

The actual events depicted in this book unfolded over many years rather than in the compressed time frame used for Valerie's story.

Table of Contents

Acknowledgments

Kevin Bosley and Cheryl Burkhardt provided valuable comments on some early chapters. Fellow writer Mary Ann Crimi provided excellent suggestions and nourished my writer's spirit with encouragement. Sally Foran of the Writers' Bloc gave insightful guidance, and I thank her.

Alex Liazos, Barbara Medlock, Richard Quinney, and Diane Turan kindly read an early, rough manuscript. Alex Liazos allowed me to draw on his biography, *Twelve Days in Vietnam,* for a character in my novel and graciously read through two versions of my manuscript. Thank you, Alex. Barb Medlock provided excellent insights and encouraged me to flesh out Valerie's mother. That character benefits from Barb's feedback. Richard Quinney encouraged me to trust myself in making literary decisions, a valuable piece of advice. Diane Turan remained supportive throughout my project, and I thank her for that and for her advice about medical issues in my writing.

Jan Cunning read my final draft. I'm grateful for her perceptive editorial comments and keen insights. My manuscript benefits from her thoughtful read and encouraging critique. Thank you.

My respect and gratitude go to two former members of the military with whom I consulted. I salute and honor Terry Nathan Turan (Army Sergeant E-5. 11B40, 1st Battalion-27th Regiment of the 25th Infantry Division) who saw active combat in Vietnam and advised my portrayals of Vietnam Veterans. Thank you Beverly Cunning Galatas (U.S. Air Force, Master Sergeant) for help with military jargon.

I did my best to incorporate all the excellent advice and suggestions. Any errors, however, rest entirely on my shoulders.

My fondest regards go to Marty Cunning who provided some intriguing suggestions and who never (or almost never) complained about sharing me with the characters in my book.

Prologue - March 1, 2002

I GASP AS MY BLOOD enters the syringe. Kurt had inserted a needle into my arm and pulled the plunger back.

"The blood means I found your vein," he tells me. I watch him remove his trigger finger. "Valerie, are you sure you want to do this?"

It's a good question, one I'd rather not face. As I struggle to form an answer, my mind retreats from the decision I need to make and goes to last June when, on the longest day of the year, a praying mantis walked into and became ensnared in a spider web stretched across the upper-right corner of the window outside my bedroom. I sprang from my reading chair intent on freeing the large, green insect but saw how its struggles had wrapped spider silk around it, straight-jacket tight, pinning its prayerful arms to its body. As I wondered if freeing the mantis would mean a slow death by starvation with its predatory arms no longer able to grab food, a spider crept out from beneath the window's frame and injected poison into its captive. Gruesome death, yes, but quicker than starving and less painful after the venomous fangs.

The spider bit, retreated, and assessed the mantis's decline several times before the captured insect's triangular head stopped all movement. Energized by the paralysis of its victim, the spider crawled about its upcoming meal encasing it in sticky threads-of-silk packaging.

My thoughts return to the needle in my arm, and I wrestle with a web of reasons for and against doing this narcotic.

PART I

SOME SAY the world will end in fire,
Some say in icc.

Robert Frost, *Harper's Magazine*, 1920

Ch. 1 – About Two Months Earlier

AS I WAIT FOR MY BOSS to approve the distribution of a memorandum summarizing the network of mergers he established since last spring, I look out my window on the 21st floor feeling trapped. The winter wind off Lake Erie sends mild tremors through the building and punches at the windowpane. I picture myself from outside where I must look like a person suspended in a web-like matrix of similarly sized openings spread throughout the building. At age 25, I am cornered with nowhere to go and pinned to this private office space with its grass-textured, rice-papered walls.

I am a perk in corporate lingo, which means I work for one man, the corporation's Executive Vice President. His other perks include stock options and a company-owned vehicle even though his salary, much higher than mine, means he can afford to buy his car. Although I'm paid well, I'm still riding public transport while I save up to buy a car.

I can't complain, though. My salary as a perk allowed me to buy furniture and move away from my parents' home last September. I love my new neighborhood even though it wasn't my first choice. I wanted to live in the suburb where many of the University Circle students and medical clinicians live, but my applications for apartments there weren't successful. Maybe it was because I'm an Administrative Assistant, a glorified secretary, which kept me from getting an apartment in that area. However, when I entered the borderland suburb between my desired neighborhood and the northeastern edges of the city, I found an affordable one-bedroom apartment in an aging, three-story walkup. The crime and unemployment rates are higher here than in the neighborhood I preferred, but this interstitial area isn't as bad as where I grew up. It's a step in the right direction, a step away from my parents.

When my computer dings, indicating the arrival of an email, I turn away from the office window. The message is from Tom, an art student I met before I dropped out of college. He had accompanied me when I looked for an apartment. Although he appears a bit unconventional with his purple-streaked hair, he's stable and plans to design light fixtures or some other useful, industrial product when he graduates. He not only helped me find my apartment but assisted with the move, unpacked boxes, and hung curtains. He wants to know if we can get together during the upcoming Christmas holidays, but I haven't seen him since Thanksgiving and don't respond to the email.

I spent Thanksgiving with Tom's family, a family that contrasted with what I'm used to. Usually, I sit with my mother and father on holidays, our heads bowed down and focused on our plates. Tom's family began the Thanksgiving meal with heads bowed in prayer, and after saying "amen," they talked about favorite sports, restaurants, cable TV programs, and celebrities. There's little talk at my family's table, but Dad's belching and noises of displeasure fill the silence as he washes food down with beer or booze. No one at Tom's table drank alcohol. Tom's home, so different and foreign to my own, made navigating the unfamiliar terrain difficult, and I watched his mom, dad, sister and brother-in-law as if viewing them through some sort of television screen. They didn't appear real to me.

After dinner, Tom kept looking my way and grinning as I helped pack up the turkey and other leftovers. Later, when his family gathered in the television room to watch a classic, black-and-white romance, I sat on the couch next to Tom. He put his arm around my shoulder and pulled me close in a proprietary manner. When he drove me home after the movie, I insisted I needed time to myself and darted from his car before he could propose coming up to my apartment with me. I consider Tom a close friend and am not physically attracted to him, but he wants more.

My dash away from Tom, a sure sign of what I do not want, jars against an awareness that Tom and his family are what I *should* want. I *should* want to encourage Tom who would probably give me an engagement ring and then the wedding band. I *should* want a secure home married to someone like Tom, and I *should* desire to have children with a stable man.

Now, a month later, a month during which I only talked with Tom by phone a couple of times, I still don't understand why I stopped seeing him and decide against responding to his current email. Yeah, I'm a coward for not telling him to his face that I'm not right for him, but I don't know who or what is right for me. I also fear I'll give in to what he wants of me if we get together. Surely something's wrong with me because I feel like the only young person who doesn't know how to get what they want from life.

My boss calls out, "Valerie, go ahead and distribute those memos." It's the task I've been anticipating, and it rescues me from thinking about Tom.

"Yes, sir, I'm on my way." I grab the envelopes at attention on my desk and head into the gridwork of halls connecting the company's various departments. It's winter solstice, and the cold I felt when I stood at my window follows me into the hallways. As I pass the elevators, I hear a "Bong" and then a smooth "Hiss" from doors sliding open. The Chairman of the Board of Directors steps out and says, "Hello, Sunshine."

I do not see anyone else in the hallway.

"You walk such a straight, fine line, my friend."

I tense up. The Chair has a lot of power, and I need to watch what I say and do. "Oh, sorry, sir. I didn't know you were talking to me."

"What a lovely day, and your straightforward walk and fine bearing bear that out." His grandfatherly face looks happy and content as he chuckles over his comment.

"Yes, sir, it sure is a lovely day." My comment makes his eyes light up. "I'm afraid I need to leave you, if that's okay. I need to drop off these memos pronto."

"Okay, Sunshine, you carry on." He makes a gesture like he's tipping a hat, does an about face, and walks away. As he travels the corridor, he does a little jig, going right and then left. His quiet mirth continues a few moments before he reins it in, turns to look back at me with a grin, and disappears around the corner. "Sunshine," he called me "Sunshine," but I am not "Sunshine."

I'm "slut," "whore," "freakin' little bitch," and worse. Those awful names missiled out from my father's feral-looking mouth, lips snarled back to expose fang-like teeth. When I was small, I spent a lot of time in my room to avoid Dad's anger and the awful names he called me. I curled up in the corner of my room and escaped into books featuring girl protagonists who were adventurous and independent. Later, as a teen, I posted the words from a Robert Frost poem over my desk and read them often. In place of the isolation, alienation, depression, and despair that most reviewers of the poem discussed, I discovered fortitude and resilience. The opening line, "I have been one acquainted with the night," trumpeted triumph from a person who "outwalked the further city light," a person who knew how to be alone, wrestle with darkness, and survive.

My room not only flourished with characters from children's authors and poems by Frost but with ideas written by others, with photos in *National Geographic,* with stereo music carrying a beat that matched the heart rate, and even with televised home runs hit into bleachers. Such artifacts in my youth served as points on a mariner's compass, and they all suggested other directions to travel if only I could journey beyond "the further city light."

After delivering the memos and returning to my desk, I am dismayed that I haven't journeyed very far. My attempt at getting a college degree failed, and I am pinned down and stuck in an office job with no hope of advancement. The Chairman's single word, "Sunshine," invokes the optimism I felt before entering a university, but such a positive sense of who I could be cannot find anchorage among all the rocky names my father had hurled into the depths of my soul. Instead of gaining purchase in solid ground, the Chair's nickname for me pinballs against the terrible ones from Dad and threatens to set off an avalanche of buried emotions. Although I cannot imagine going anywhere desirable, everything inside me wants to move fast.

It's clear that as much as I want to find a better place for myself in the world and embrace a positive view of who I am, I carry too much negative baggage to accomplish anything worthwhile. How could the Chairman of my company look at me and see anything positive enough to remind him of sunshine?

I look at the time and am relieved to see it's close enough to my lunch hour to leave the office. I need to get outside for a walk and dispel some of the nervous energy pulsing through me. I grab my coat, slide into it, and walk toward the elevators. I pause near the lunchroom to pull on a knit hat, scarf, and gloves, and hear some coworkers talking about their Secret Santa gifts. The talk about gifts makes me smile as I place my hand inside my coat pocket to touch the secret present I placed there, one not for a co-worker.

I take the elevator to the first floor and head for the south side of the building where an exit leads to nearby restaurants and shops. Foot traffic is light on this cold, winter day. I look for the silhouette of a man who often takes shelter outside the door, out of the way of pedestrians, and wonder if he'll be there on such a harsh wintry day.

The windows on either side of the revolving door are frosted, and I do not see the man at first. Then, two silhouettes take shape in the icy glass. His huddled form, the one I'm looking for, becomes overshadowed by another figure. The unexpected shape moving toward him is of a young, slender woman bundled up against the cold. Even though she's wearing a knit hat and scarf, I can see her pleasant face and some dark, shiny hair hanging out from the hat.

The woman seems to be standing close to the man I seek, but she isn't as she appears. He is outside; she moves inside the building and materializes into someone I know. I am that woman reflected in the glass. The attractive face mirrored back to me doesn't fit with my negative self-image, and it takes time to adjust to the fact that I am looking at my reflection. I refocus my vision so that I see only the man outside.

The man crouches at the base of this thirty-story structure where business professionals, in their office finery, pass by. He is in a ragged, olive-drab field jacket with a camo watch cap pulled snug over his forehead and ears. His desert-style jungle boots are worn but serviceable for this cold weather. Near him rests a piece of cardboard with the roughly written words, "Homeless Veteran." I reach into my pocket for the wool socks I found at an Army-Navy surplus store.

"Hey, Sarge," is all I say as I go through the revolving doors and place the socks on the stone in the alcove where he crouches. I also leave an envelope containing some cash and a gift certificate for a nearby sandwich shop. I've learned that this man doesn't want to talk, and he rarely acknowledges anyone. I've greeted him often, but this is the first time he responds. His eyes raise to meet mine. Our eye contact happens so quickly that I'm startled before he looks away. Although I'm pleased by the man's brief recognition, it reminds me of my interaction with the Chair.

I turn and walk away from him to wander the cold, snow-covered streets laid out between concrete office buildings. I move rapidly as if someone or something is in pursuit, but I'm not sure if I'm evading or closing in on what's disturbing me.

At home that evening, I look for a task to distract me. I'm still feeling unsettled and yank the laundry basket from my closet. With dirty clothes and detergent on one hip, I leave my apartment, lock the door, enter the third-floor corridor, and head for the basement-level washers and dryers.

In the hallway, I hear the sounds of neighbors chatting in one apartment while "*jingle bell, jingle bell, jingle bell rock*" sings out from another unit's audio system. I pick up the aromas of nutmeg and cinnamon from someone's kitchen. It's good to allow the holiday sensations scattered throughout my apartment building provide comfort after my trying day.

As soon as I pass the entryway on the first floor, a blast of cold air spirits around me when a young couple with a toddler throws open the door and enters. The elevated mood of husband and wife echoes in the stairwell as they talk excitedly about their daughter's upcoming Christmas. They don't notice me standing on the basement stairs below them as they climb up from the entryway.

The woman asks, "Did you see how little Maggie's eyes lit up when she saw those elves?"

"Yeah," her husband answers. "And she wasn't even afraid of Santa. I can't wait to give Granny the photo of Maggie on Santa's lap."

After the young family goes through the doors separating the first floor from the stairwell, I look up and out the window next to the entrance door where a Marley-like face, carved in the building's stone alcove, scowls. An icicle cracks off its countenance, daggers through a ghostly swirl of snowflakes, and stabs a shoveled-up embankment of snow. I turn away, hug my laundry basket closer, and continue to the basement where music and laughter pour out of the custodian's sublevel apartment. I also hear a buzzer down the hall, inside the laundry area, announcing the end of a cycle. The door to the laundry room, usually closed and locked, stands wide open.

When I reach the door, I see the custodian's wife, Alice, removing clothes from a dryer. I met Alice and her husband, John, several months ago when I moved in. They appear to be around 50 years old, about the same age as my parents. Alice's long, graying hair is pulled back, and she wears a colorful tunic over billowy, black pants.

"Hey, Valerie."

"Hey," I mumble in return.

"Haven't seen you much since you moved in," Alice says as she snaps out a bath towel and begins folding it.

"Yeah. I've been busy unpacking and working but glad to have a long weekend break for Christmas." I put my laundry basket down in front of one of the washers and ask, "How have you been?"

"I'm fine," Alice says before adding, "Hey, how's your boyfriend?"

"Oh, you must mean Tom, the man who helped me move in. Well . . ," I begin but find I can't say more because my eyes tear up. I stop loading the washer and concentrate on not crying. The mention of Tom brings to mind everything that happened during the day. I'm at a loss about why I am feeling overwhelmed and shaky. Maybe I'm just tired.

"Oh, . . . oh dear," Alice says as she puts a partially folded washcloth down and places her hand on my shoulder.

I close my eyes, exhale and shake my head to clear up my thinking. "It's okay, Alice. It's just that," I begin to say but my voice catches in my throat, and I stop talking.

"You poor dear. Here, scoot over." I step back as Alice finishes taking the clothes from my basket, loads them into the washer, and measures out some detergent. I try to jam in a few quarters, but my hands fumble and I keep dropping them. Alice picks up the coins and puts them in the slot. When she pushes the money in, I hear the quarters drop and the machine begins to fill with water.

"Sorry, Alice. I'm not sure what came over me."

She gives me a gentle hug. "Everyone feels stressed around the holidays, dear. I'm sure everything will be fine."

I take a step back, raise my head, and wipe my nose on my sleeve. "Yeah, . . . yeah, I'm sure you're right."

Alice looks away for a moment before turning to me and saying, “Valerie, I have something that might take your mind off things. Wanna see it?”

Ch. 2 - Through the Access Door

IN RESPONSE TO ALICE'S question about seeing something, I say "Yeah, sure, why not."

"Okay, then, come with me," Alice says as she grabs a set of keys lying next to her folded clothes. She leaves the laundry room, and I follow her across the hallway to what appears to be a short cupboard. As she unlocks the cabinet door, she says, "John and I usually enter this area from our unit, but this old access door works just as well. Wait until I switch on the lights, then go through to the landing and take the stairs."

I watch Alice scrunch down and evaporate from view when she passes through the small gap in the wall into darkness. I stare down at the black opening, smell dust-scented air as it comes up and moves past me, and listen to the soft soles of Alice's sandals as they meet metal steps. A few moments after I no longer hear her tread on the stairs, there's a crackling sound as a bank of fluorescent lights hum to life.

Alice yells up, "Well, you coming?"

I stoop, poke my head into the doorway, and step through to a small landing. Below is an underworld platoon of mops, buckets, plungers, and other custodial implements. I see no reason to hesitate and go down the metal stairway into a cavernous cellar. Near the bottom of the stairs, an ancient boiler converts water into steam and deploys it to an army of radiators posted throughout the building.

Alice walks away from the sentry-like boiler to the end of the sub-basement farthest from the access door. I follow her past oversized stones embedded in the cellar walls and enter an area that is dimly lit by the fluorescent lights. Clammy air and a musky odor tug at some long-buried memory and stir up flashes of fear.

A creepy feeling seeps into me, and I begin to back away. "Alice, I have to . . . uh . . . get back to my laundry." When I turn to go, something hairy moves across my left cheek. I yelp, leap back a step, rub my cheek to make sure it's uninjured, and look for whatever brushed against me.

Alice peers from me to the overhead heating pipes. "Oh, there you are," she sings out.

Alice's calm manner and relaxed voice do not reassure me. The twitching tail dangling from a spidery network of insulated steam pipes over my head makes me uncomfortable.

Alice asks, "Staying warm up there, are you?"

At the sound of Alice's voice, the tail begins jerking in quick, short movements. I look up over the pipe with the tail hanging from it and see two yellow points of light. As my eyes adjust to the darkness, I make out a furry body sprawled along the insulated tube, forelegs embracing the heat. Alice gets a footstool, reaches up, retrieves the hairy critter, and hugs it to her chest. She removes a collar with a bell on it from her pocket and puts the band on the neck of what is either a cat or kitten. "This bell should make it easier to find you."

Then, Alice turns to me. "She's a stray. She was hanging around out in the snow mewling for days, so I brought her inside." Alice, still nuzzling the cat close to her body, runs a hand along its coat. "This little one sure was hungry and ate through a big bowl of kibble in a few hours."

"It's pretty," I tell Alice.

"She's a calico. Cat fanciers love their tri-colored coats and claim these cats bring good luck to their owners." Alice hugs the furry kitten to her shoulder, walks in a circle with a bit of a bounce in her step, and makes the cooing sounds used by mothers to soothe babies. "If the building's owner finds her here, I'll be in trouble, and he'll take her to the city pound."

Alice looks at me and pleads, "Is there any way you can keep her until I find a permanent home? I already take care of three cats and can't add another one to our family."

"Geez, Alice, I don't know." I feel cornered by Alice's request and unsettled by a sub-basement atmosphere that's triggering unwanted images and emotions. I begin thinking about men with unzipped pants standing near a furnace and need to get out of this basement boiler room so I agree, "Well . . . okay . . . if it's only for a little while."

Alice doesn't register my alarm. Instead, she grins and pushes the wee creature into my arms where it gets comfortable and begins purring. While I hedge about the wisdom of taking the calico as a temporary roommate, Alice retrieves the cat's possessions from under a small table.

We leave the basement, forget about our laundry, and head up to my apartment where Alice creates what she calls, "a kitten-friendly place." A litter box gets placed in the hall near the bathroom, and the bowls go on a placemat next to the kitchen table. One bowl gets filled with water and another one with dry cat food. She places the cat's toy on my bookshelf. The poinsettia I won at the company Christmas party is toxic to pets, according to Alice, so she moves the plant to the bathroom and closes the door.

"Alice, that's my only Christmas decoration."

Alice ignores my protest and says, "John will be wondering where the hell I went, so I'd better leave. I'll come back in a day or so to see how you two are doing." She gives me a hug and exits without giving me time to reconsider or even discuss the arrangement.

After the whirlwind of Alice leaves, I look down at the furry being. "You have a temporary place to stay, and I'll give you food and water but otherwise you're on your own." My comment helps me remain unattached since I'm not sure it's a good idea to keep this kitten even for a few days.

The creature, not yet grown but clearly beyond kittenhood, scampers away setting off its new belled collar. It tries to climb a tall basket but vanishes when the floor decoration topples over and captures the feline inside. The calico-possessed basket begins scooting across the black-and-white checkerboard floor in sporadic, yet determined, chessboard moves. A muffled bell goes "Ding" with each move of the woven, rook-like shape.

Exasperated by the change in my intent to remain detached from this animal, I pick up the overturned basket and grab the cat. My first inclination is to slam it on the floor for being stupid as my father did to me when I was small and did what he thought was dumb. I have grasped its tiny body just under its front legs with both my hands and hold it at shoulder height ready to punish it. Its legs dangle down, and its body stretches out as it goes still and stares me in the eye. Eyeball to eyeball, I think back to how Alice hugged this small cat and made cooing sounds. I break off my gaze, close my eyes, and hesitate. The kitten starts to squirm, and my arms begin to quiver. Then, I take a quick breath in preparation to teach this cat a lesson, but my hands begin shaking. I should discipline this cat, but I can't. I lower my hands to waist level, open them up, and release the cat.

She tumbles a short two feet to the floor in innocence of any harm and resumes exploring her new terrain. For me, old memories shrapnel out from long-dark places. I slide down to the floor, close my eyes, and sit. I wrap my arms around my knees and pull them close to my chest. Strange images flash through my mind. They include a fiery-hot furnace room, but it's not the one through Alice's access door. The one in my memory smells of sweat and contains fists, belts, and pants unzipped. When the images stop and I open my eyes, I see a calico cat on straightened legs, back arched, like she's fighting an invisible yet ferocious foe.

"Good girl," I tell her. "You get 'em, tiger."

Ch. 3 - Names and Labels

TWO DAYS LATER, I'M PACKING an overnight bag when I hear a knock at the door. It's Alice carrying a metal box and a plate of brownies wrapped in bright, red cellophane with a sticker proclaiming, "Alice's Special Treats." She sets the "Treats" and a tin of holiday cookies on the coffee table in the living room before giving me a hug. "Merry Christmas, Valerie"

Before I can thank her for the baked goods, she pulls a sandwich bag from her pocket, opens it, and sprinkles catnip on the floor.

"I brought goodies for you, too," she tells the feline as it leaps down from the windowsill overlooking the street.

The cat catches the scent, goes over to the herb, and rolls in the dried leaves. The catnip energizes her, and she begins rocketing skyward on stiffened legs. Her antics, so playful and comical, send me and Alice into bursts of laughter.

Alice wipes tears from her face as she kicks off her sandals and curls up in one of the chairs by the window. "How ya doing, Val, on this Christmas Eve day?"

The question reminds me of my upcoming visit to my parents. "I'm okay, I guess," is all I can say as I take the other chair in the front of the room.

My less-than-enthusiastic reply catches Alice's attention, and she studies me a moment. "Can I ask what your plans are for Christmas?"

"I'm going to my parents," I tell her. I'm not looking forward to the visit, don't want to say more, and change topics to one that will short-circuit any more talk about the holiday. "In fact, I was packing an overnight bag and need to catch a bus in an hour. I want to get there before dark."

"Oh. I won't stay long. I wanted to see how you and the cat are doing."

The feline, aware that Alice was talking about her, leaps into Alice's lap and begins kneading her belly. Alice tickles the underside of its chin, and the kitten settles down. A gentle smile spreads across Alice's face, and she starts humming.

I look at the cellophane-wrapped brownies and ask, "Alice, what does the label about special treats mean?"

Alice hums awhile longer before saying, "You may find the brownies a bit dry. I baked an herb into them."

"An herb?" My brow scrunches up.

Alice studies me a moment and says, "Val, you may not like them. John calls them magic brownies because they make tension disappear."

"Are you telling me the brownies contain marijuana?"

Alice doesn't respond but keeps petting the cat in her lap.

"I tried smoking pot with a group of classmates once during college but it made me cough a lot and then feel scared. I didn't like the feeling."

After giving some thought to what I said, Alice tells me, "These brownies won't make you cough and will let you try a lighter hit, one that doesn't come on too fast."

"You know, I want to try that."

"Good. When you do eat one or two, you may want the cookies as munchies." Alice looks at me with an impish grin before adding, "John and I wonder if you have plans for New Year's Eve."

I'm a bit embarrassed to admit that I don't have plans and am reluctant to tell her.

When I don't answer right away, Alice says "Look, if you're free, we'd love to see you. We're having a few friends over. Nothing formal. Come any time after 7:00 if you can make it."

It's great having an invitation and a place to go for the holiday. Since I didn't answer Tom's email, my only other option is a dull evening with my parents.

"Great. I'd love to come."

"By the way," Alice says as she puts the cat on the floor, slides her sandals back on, and gets ready to leave, "did you name the cat?"

"Uh . . . no. Should I?"

"Only if you want. No big deal." She pats my arm, opens the door, and exits into the hallway.

"Bye, Alice," I say and then step into the hall to tell her, "See you in a week."

I return to packing my overnight bag and know that naming the cat is a bad idea if I don't plan on keeping her. I'm not sure why, but I find myself spending time thinking about possible names. The most prominent name I know uses the initials, J and P. JP, one of my father's coworkers, began visiting my dad one winter when I was five years old. On a spring evening several months later, we sat outdoors when JP took my hands, got up, and swung me around while Mom and Dad stayed motionless at the picnic table. I laughed as I looked into JP's smiling face and knew I was safe because I could trust that he wouldn't let his grip on me slip. When JP needed a break and led me to the outdoor table, I snuggled next to him on the bench opposite my mother and father.

After JP left, I saw Father's eyes grow mean, and he snarled, "JP, JP, JP," as he slapped me several times on the side of my head. The last hit was hard enough to make my ear ring, so the next time JP visited, I sat next to my father. I ignored JP the best that I could, but I saw his puzzled look every time his questioning eyes sought mine. My eyes had turned vacant, and I stayed seated next to the tyrant who ruled my life.

Other names belong to people I keep away from memory. *What were those men's names, the gym teacher and the custodian?* A misty sense of a memory more than any actual recall informs me of the two creepy men who lured me out of the elementary school gymnasium into the adjacent boiler room to . . . to what?

I can't remember more than that so I refocus my attention on naming the cat. Inspired by Alice's hippie appearance, I recall a name from a 1960s television rerun in which a San Francisco "flower child" named her hamster, Bean, which was short for Being or Be-In or something similar. The calico cat begins batting at a tag hanging from my overnight bag, and I divert her attention by taking a shoelace and dangling it in front of her. She leaps after it as I flip the string around in the air, and I regret having to leave her tonight.

"See you tomorrow, Bean," I whisper as I lock the door to my unit. *Geez! Did I just name the cat?*

"Thanks for the gift, Alice," I mumble to myself, "and I don't mean the brownies."

Ch. 4 - The Spiritually Dead

MY TRIGGER FINGER RESTS ON a chemical-based, self-defense canister when I enter the pedestrian passage that goes under the transit-station tracks near my parents' home. On the bus to the transfer station and then the train across town, I had thought about keeping the cat and wondered about Alice's upcoming party, but now I need to pay attention while on this isolated sidewalk under the train tracks.

The walkway is ten feet above the road and bordered on one side by a cement wall that emits a faint odor of urine, a smell that festers strong in the summer months. A metal pipe fence runs along the side that drops off to traffic, and I'm relieved to see no one else is present. When I'm halfway through the underpass, a train passes overhead. The clacking wheels and a vibrating hum make me shiver. The sounds warn of something menacing, so I grip the can of pepper-based spray tighter and speed up my pace.

When I emerge from that dark passage, I remove my finger from the self-defense canister and begin an uphill, three-quarter mile trek to my parents' street. Mid-sized factories and some warehouses on my left are separated from the sidewalk by a chain-link fence topped with barbed wire. The sidewalk is nothing more than a small ledge between fence and road and provides little distance from the icy slush tossed up by cars and trucks. A chilly wind sends a dissonant rattle along the fence and reminds me not to let my guard down in this industrial section of town.

At the top of the incline, I turn left onto a street where homes face storage lots and small factories on the opposite side of the road. I can see the billboard next to my childhood home a few blocks away. My parents' house sits next to an undeveloped piece of land that once provided a weed-infested jungle for me and a couple of childhood friends. I know the summer sting of thistle and the unpleasant taste of milkweed juice stuck to tiny fingers. I climbed the support structure inside the V-shaped billboard like it was a jungle gym. My hands retain the memory of hard, angular beams that pressed red lines into my hands when I climbed to the top and peered down over the enticing ads. This evening, the billboard features a winking Santa Claus, his gloved hand holding a frosted mug of cola, while weeds bent dead by snow surround the base of the structure.

Father's car rests idly in the driveway. He never offers to pick me up.

Mother sees my approach as I make my way up the shoveled drive to the back door, and she lets me in. When we hug, I feel her tension. It's my first sign that something's not right in the house tonight.

"How was the trip over?"

"Quiet. Not too many people were onboard." It's good to step inside after the chilly walk from the train.

"Better safe than sorry."

Mom's response reflects her reliance on trite phrases to replace thoughtful conversation. Her style of speech is something I call fortune-cookie talk. "You made your bed, now lie in it," is one of her favorite sayings.

I take a moment to enjoy the warmth in the kitchen, but I am unable to feel safe inside this house. Dad's belligerent responses to a television news reporter rise up from the basement and throw an uneasy undertone into the kitchen.

"Something smells good," I say in an attempt to lessen the impact of Dad's anger.

"Oh, roast chicken and baked potatoes. Nothing special."

I remove my gloves and hat, check that my self-defense canister remains tucked into one coat pocket, and shove the hat and gloves into the other pocket. Then, I remove my coat and put it with my overnight bag on a chair in the living room before returning to the kitchen to help Mom. "How's the holiday going?"

"Okay, I guess. I went to church earlier, but the scripture unsettled me."

"Why?"

Mom takes a few moments to consider her answer, an unusual behavior on her part. "Well, the passage was about the birth of Christianity."

Something's very different tonight. Mom always accepts without question what those in authority say. "Okay, the birth of Christianity parallels the birth of Christ. I don't get what's strange."

"Well, the scripture came from Matthew, the verses where Jesus encouraged a disciple to leave a 'spiritually dead' relative."

A loud "Fuck that," invades the kitchen. Dad's not happy when he hears the news about a large, energy corporation doing "creative accounting." Father lost part of his pension fund when the energy company's stock tumbled from over ninety dollars a share to twenty-six cents.

Mom ignores the outburst from below and changes the topic, "Anyway, I have a gift for you, and I want to tell you something important."

Exasperated by the change in topic and by a breach of our agreement, I whine, "Mom, we agreed on not exchanging gifts."

"It's not exactly a gift, but it is something I want you to have."

Mom removes a small box from her pocket, opens it, and pulls out her high school ring. "I worked during my senior year to buy this ring."

"It's lovely, Mom."

Mom sighs. "This ring meant so much to me at one time. When I graduated, I dreamed about being a single, working woman like Marlo Thomas in *That Girl*, but my dream lasted only a couple of months."

"What happened?"

"Your father returned from Vietnam and asked me to marry him. I worried about him while he was there, and he seemed robbed of his youth or something when he got back. I wanted to help him and agreed to get married. Then, you came along nine months later."

Mom goes quiet while I grow apprehensive over what's going on.

From the basement, Dad yells, "Those fucking bastards." A TV newscaster discusses the recently signed trade agreement giving American corporations, investors, and banks access to 80 million Vietnamese citizens. "What the hell did we all fight and die for?" Dad's anger escalates.

"Mom, are you okay?" The question brings her back to our conversation.

"Oh." Mom clears her head with a few shakes and whispers, "I guess I replaced my school ring with wedding bands."

"I'm sorry you had to give up your dream, Mom."

"Well, it's all water under the bridge now."

Mom stares a moment at the ring before putting it back in the box and snapping the lid shut with a brisk, business-like movement.

With the same briskness, she says, "I can't stay here any longer. Today's sermon about leaving the spiritually dead helped me decide, and I called my sister this morning."

Mom's sister, my Aunt Cora, is ten years younger than Mom and ten years older than I am. We don't see her or her husband Pete very often because they live a four-hour drive away. Once I'm able to get a car, I plan to visit more and get to know them better. They do not visit here because Dad dislikes Uncle Pete.

"Why'd you phone Aunt Cora?"

"I took her up on her offer to move back to West Virginia and live with her and Pete. Pete's picking me up two days after Christmas while your father is at work."

"Geez, Mom. I don't know what to say."

"Valerie, silence is golden; anyway, the plan is set in stone." Mom's use of two platitudes indicates that she's through talking and I won't learn more, but it's clear that she plans to leave Dad, and I'm happy for that.

Mom hands me the box with the ring in it, turns away, and begins plating the chicken and potatoes.

I put the box in my jeans pocket and feel its pressure against my hip, an uncomfortable reminder about my having dropped out of school without a degree and without a college ring.

I watch Mom carve the chicken and hide the butcher knife. Hidden cutlery signifies that Dad's been drinking a lot and may be dangerous.

Mom straightens up and calls out, "Paul, dinner's ready."

The basement television clicks off, but Dad's volcanic swearing continues as he moves up the stairs and erupts into the kitchen like unwanted molten lava. Some of his whiskey flows up and out of the glass when he maneuvers his drink from an unsteady hand to the table. His hands, made red and rough from the cleaning fluids he uses at work, shake. He does a two-step, rebalances, plops onto a chair, and immediately begins filling his plate as Mom and I take our places at the table. His belches and grunts form a Richter-scale warning about his volatile state.

Dad usually bolts his food down and then leaves Mom and me alone, but tonight Dad sermonizes about soldiers he knew who lost their lives or were injured. He isn't happy about the current friendly trade relations with Vietnam.

I say in as gentle a voice as I can, "Maybe the world is safer from war if our enemy is an economic partner."

Dad looks at me like I'm the enemy and slurs, "Why weren't they made a . . . PARTNER," spit flies from Dad's mouth, "*before* soldiers died?"

I put my fork down and stare at food I no longer want to eat. Father makes valid points, but there's no way to talk with him in his drunken, angry state.

"God damn it, Valerie. For Christ's sake, use your fuckin' brain for once."

The verbal attack makes my body tighten and my hands curl into fists. My mouth, in an unbidden motion, opens. Before I can stop myself, I yell back, "For crying out loud, Dad, it's Christmas Eve. Stop taking the Lord's name in vain!"

My eyes widen at the sound of my defiance. Terror and bile rise in my throat, because I know that any act of insurgence provokes severe retaliation from this madman. My heart and breathing launch off like racehorses out of the starting gate. I want to run.

I get up while Dad tries to stand but falls back against the wall. I do not run but move around the table and grip my father by the throat. I relish seeing fear dart through his eyes since I have always wanted to hurt the man who hurt me. I tighten my grasp around his neck and smell his sour whiskey breath as he gasps for air. He tries to grab my wrists, but his drunken hands flounder. He needs them for balance. He begins to slide down the wall, and the weight of him pulls at my arms. I push into him to keep him semi-upright, and my hands tighten around his throat.

"Valerie, stop," Mom yells as she pounds my back. "Let him go."

I release him, and he slides to the floor.

I turn away and hurry to the living room, pick up my jacket and overnight bag, and get ready to leave by the front door. There's no way I'm staying here tonight. I hear my father scramble to his feet in the kitchen and begin to come after me. My hand seizes the doorknob, but I can't escape. Dad clutches my hair and yanks my head back. A fierce resolve to get even with me replaces his alcoholic languor. I drop everything but my jacket and fumble inside the pocket for my can of pepper-based spray.

Dad spins me around so we are face-to-face. He lets me go so he can take a step back and ready a fist. I jerk the self-defense canister out of my jacket, put a finger on the trigger, cover my mouth with my free hand, and spray.

Dad's fist misses my face, and he begins coughing and rubbing his eyes. I jerk my overnight bag off the floor, throw open the front door, and rush outside. Father roars out obscenities as I move to the sidewalk.

"You fuckin' bitch. Don't ever come back here."

I cross the street, stop, and look back to make sure Dad isn't in pursuit. I pull my jacket on, turn away, and hustle through the now dark streets back to the transit station. During my trek home, a trip I hardly remember, I stew about how much I hate that man, my father.

I exit the bus outside my apartment a few minutes after midnight, key into the building, and climb to the third floor. Bean meows from inside as I work the lock to the unit, and then she rubs against my leg when I enter. I put my bag on the floor, remove my coat, toss it aside, and pick up Bean. Then, I create a gentle, relaxing glow by turning on some nightlights. I put Bean down, and she follows me into my bedroom where I pull out some sweats. When I remove my jeans, the box with Mom's high school ring drops out of the pocket where I had shoved it. That ring symbolizes independence and pride in an educational accomplishment that I can't embrace for myself. I hide the ring behind some spare linens in the closet where I'm unlikely to see it. I shut the linen door and snuggle into my sweats.

In order to take my mind off that ring and what happened with my father, I unwrap one of Alice's special treats. They are dry, as Alice warned they would be, so I make some coffee, spike it with Kahlua, dunk one end of the "special treat" in the java, and chew on the wet pastry. After finishing one brownie, I take Bean in my arms and feel her purring sounds of contentment as I unwind enough to go to bed and try to sleep.

Bean wakes me on Christmas morning by nuzzling my head as I lie in bed. Although I'm alone on the holiday rather than with family, I do not feel lonely or isolated. Bean is nearby, and I hear John and Alice calling "Merry Christmas" to neighbors as their shovels scrape a light layer of snow from the sidewalk.

I sit up, rub Bean under her chin, and slide my feet into slippers. The radiators tick as heat surges through them to warm my apartment. I walk the hallway from my bedroom to the kitchen where I turn on a burner to reheat some coffee left from the previous night. A few minutes later, I go to the front window with a coffee mug in one hand and a brownie in the other. I see sunshine glistening on fresh snow and watch Bean stretch out in a patch of sunlit warmth on the carpet.

John and Alice are below, and I tap on the window. When Alice looks up, I dip the brownie in my steaming mug of coffee and raise the "special treat" in a morning salute. She lifts her shovel overhead like she's waving a flag of victory and smiles.

Ch. 5 - New Year's Eve

I SEE MY FATHER'S FACE as I stand before the bathroom mirror. When I see his features in my face, I often think, "*I hate you*," but I'm never sure if that hostile sentiment is directed at my Dad or to me.

Tonight, before going to Alice's party, I try to see myself as people outside my family might see me. I'm petite, only five-feet, three-inches tall, and weigh 110 pounds. So, I'm short with a slender frame. My dark, chin-length hair, cut in a bob, shines. I'm average looking, not beautiful, not ugly. I don't apply much makeup because that means staying in front of the mirror looking at a face too similar to Father's, so I apply a little mascara and lip gloss then retreat from the room.

I slip out of my robe, toss it on the bed, and look through my bedroom wardrobe. My clothes, all in dark or muted tones, create a cave-like display of beiges, browns, grays, and charcoals.

I decide to dress in "I-don't-care," post-grunge attire. An oversized, black-and-white flannel shirt, cuffs turned up, goes over a long-sleeved black tee. I pull on a pair of torn, tight-fitting black jeans and cuff the pant legs up several inches. Black, high-top sneakers finish the ensemble, and the outfit will have to do. After all, Alice said the party was casual.

I toss Bean a few treats, grab a bottle of wine, and head downstairs. Outside John and Alice's apartment, I hear laughter and the voices of their guests. I hate small talk and think about leaving before anyone knows I'm there. As I deliberate over whether to knock, I hear Alice's voice rise above the chatter and decide I don't want to disappoint her.

When I knock, John opens the door allowing the scent of marijuana to drift into the hallway. John's bushy red beard, full head of hair, pudgy demeanor, and twinkling eyes remind me of a hobbit. My eyes light up in response to his, and I smile as I enter his below-ground apartment where heating pipes crisscross the ceiling.

John introduces me to Rick, a heavyset man with short blond hair, and Steve whose long ears, droopy eyes, and Fu Manchu mustache create the impression of a man with the face of a hound dog.

"Rick and Steve live in the apartment across the hall," John says. "Steve's a motorcycle mechanic. We've been friends since high school."

Alice greets me and finishes the introductions. "Steve is with his girlfriend, Pat. She's a tattoo artist. Over by the food-and-drink table in the adjoining room are two members of a local band, their girlfriends, and Kurt." She takes my bottle of wine and offers a joint. When I hesitate, Alice says "Take a light hit. You'll be fine."

I inhale a little without coughing it out and like the way it makes me feel. I settle into an overstuffed chair and listen to John and Steve talk about muscle-car engines. I chuckle as Alice and Pat roll their eyes in reaction to the masculine topic, but they soon maneuver the discussion to what music to play. I join the debate over the merits of Nickelback, 3 Doors Down, and Aerosmith until John takes charge by popping in "Sticky Fingers," a Rolling Stones CD.

Alice hands me a drink, and I sink back into the chair, listen to the music, and close my eyes. When I open them, Alice smiles and winks at me. I'm feeling content, and I like Alice's friends because they are easy to be with.

When "Moonlight Mile" begins playing and I hear its mystical guitar licks, I begin to sway along to the lyrical tune. I'm relaxed and happy. When I look into the adjacent room, Kurt smiles at me and lifts his drink.

Kurt is razor-thin like a runner or bicyclist, but something about him is unlike an outdoor athlete. He is pale rather than tanned. His deep-set eyes and pinched cheeks hint of an unwholesome activity. His blonde hair could use a trim, but his goatee frames his face well. As he engages in conversation with the band members and their girlfriends, his eyes sparkle. When he laughs at remarks made, his face transforms into one that's inviting, and I enjoy having his attention as he glances in my direction.

I get up and go to the area with food and drink, a move that puts me closer to Kurt. After I refresh my drink, I linger near Kurt and his group, but they are engaged in a conversation about guitars. I don't know anything that would allow me to join the discussion, so I don't. Instead, I look over the titles of some books and magazines on a shelf above the snack table. Recent issues of *High Times* sit alongside literature from the beat and hippie generations. I pick up a book authored by Alan Ginsberg.

Kurt comes over and takes a handful of pretzels. "Hi."

I look up from the book I'm holding.

"Aren't you Valerie, the woman who took in Alice's stray cat?"

My eyes widen. "Yikes, I hope I'm not known as the building's cat woman!"

Kurt looks to see if I'm teasing, and I grin. "Yeah, I'm Valerie, and I'm a recent convert to pet ownership."

Kurt mimics Groucho Marx by wiggling his eyebrows and pretending to hold a cigar when he says, "Alice does have her methods of finding homes for strays."

I laugh but catch something in Kurt's voice that's serious enough to make me think he isn't talking about pets.

"And, you're Kurt, right?"

"Yep, guilty on that count." He points to the book in my hand. "I like Ginsberg's poem, 'Howl.' Have you read it?"

"Yeah, Ginsberg's anger over the mistreatment of outsiders is powerful."

Kurt hesitates a moment before adding, "I wonder if John and Alice's friends are a modern version of Ginsberg's outcasts." Kurt's eyes are smiling.

"Then that would make you and me outcasts, too."

Kurt laughs. "It would."

"How are you an outsider," I begin to ask but a commotion in the main room diverts my attention. Janet, who lives across the hall from me with her boyfriend, has come in announcing in a loud, throaty voice, "I need help. I need stuff to get a bullet out of a friend."

"What?" Alice asks.

Janet continues. "When me and Mitch got home, we find a friend waitin' for us. He got a .22 in his shoulder. We gotta dig it out."

"Take him to emergency!" Alice says.

"He won't go to no hospital. Doctors call cops for gunshots. We need somethin' to sterilize stuff and some bandages. You got any?"

Everyone stares at Janet, and someone pauses the CD.

Janet looks around and fixes her attention in my and Kurt's direction. "Kurt, can you help?"

I look at Kurt who nods at Janet and puts his drink down. Janet looks at John who shrugs as he gets up and says, "Alice, I'll go with Kurt. Can you put together some supplies for Janet?"

Alice frowns and shakes her head but complies with John's request. She goes into the bathroom to gather first-aid items. Kurt touches my arm and smiles before he leaves with John.

After Janet takes off, supplies in hand, Alice apologizes. "Janet and Mitch keep bringing trouble to this building. They're hard-core drug users, and I wish John would have the building's owner evict them."

No one restarts the music, and conversations interrupted by Janet's entrance do not restart. Steve walks over, hugs Alice, and tells her, "Pat and I are leaving. I'm fed up with Mitch and Janet's bullshit and don't want my New Year's Eve spoiled."

The band members and their girlfriends feel the same and decide to go to a different party. Alice says she understands and accepts their apologies. Then, she begins gathering abandoned cups and plates while Rick and I help her.

When Rick leaves, I tell Alice, "I'm sorry about your party. I was having a great time."

Alice sighs. "Some things can't be helped." She puts a tie around the garbage bag we filled. "I saw you talking to Kurt. You two seem to hit it off."

"Yeah, I hope we did. We started talking only a few minutes before Janet dropped in."

"Her entrance was badly timed then."

"Do you know why she asked for Kurt's help?"

"Yeah. Kurt has some medical experience from the military."

"How does Janet know that?"

Alice hesitates and looks away from me. I wait for an answer.

"Kurt came back from Desert Storm with health issues. He uses some strong prescriptions for the pain and sometimes gets . . . uh . . .

painkillers from Janet and Mitch." Something about the way Alice hesitated before saying *painkillers* stirs up a mental red flag, but I ignore that internal warning.

"Mitch served overseas, too, and I guess he and Kurt sometimes talk about their deployments. Janet probably overheard them." Alice pauses and lets out a breath of air before continuing. "Valerie, Kurt's a good guy, but something's going wrong with his prescriptions." She moves away from me, and I'm not sure that she'll tell me more.

She stops moving, hesitates, and then turns back to me, "I bet you'd be good for him, Valerie."

"Alice, what about me? Would Kurt be good for me?" I pose the question to myself as much as I ask it of Alice.

Alice looks away, and I wonder about how much she knows but isn't telling me.

She asks, "Do you like him?"

"Yeah, . . . yeah, I think I do."

"It wouldn't hurt to get together and see what happens."

"I guess you're right, Alice. Hey, is there anything else I can do?"

"Nope, I'm good here."

A lot happened during the two hours I spent in John and Alice's apartment, and I want some time alone. "Well, Alice, I guess I'll head back upstairs."

I give her a hug and say, "Happy new year, Alice."

"You, too, Val. Stop by anytime, okay?"

When I arrive on the third floor and stand outside my door, I hear cries of pain from Janet and Mitch's unit a few yards away from mine.

John says, "Keep him still, dammit."

I imagine the blood and pain in that apartment before going inside my unit where I can't hear the sounds of surgery. I tune in some acoustic music on the stereo receiver, make some tea, and spike it with whiskey. The year will turn to 2002 in a half-hour so I settle near the front window where Bean jumps into my lap. I wrap one hand around the warmth coming from the mug of tea and tickle Bean's backside with my other hand. I wonder about Kurt and wish our conversation about poetry and outsiders hadn't been interrupted.

At midnight, fireworks go off in the street and a few neighbors cheer. I turn my head to watch the colorful bursts and almost do not hear a light tapping at my door. The noises send Bean bounding for the floor. I get up, too, and look through the peephole to see Kurt standing in the hallway.

When I open the door, he says "I know it's late. Do you mind if I come in?"

"No. I'd love company."

I take Kurt's jacket, toss it on the couch, and point at my whiskey-infused drink sitting on the table between two old wingback chairs. "I'm having tea spiked with whiskey. Want some?"

"Yeah, I can sure use a drink right now."

When I return from the kitchen, I see Kurt petting Bean. I put his drink next to mine and settle back into my chair. Kurt takes the other wing chair near the front windows. Icy snow pellets pepper the windowpane behind us, but the nearby radiator compensates with waves of warm air. Night lights provide a gentle glow, and we sit quietly while Bean curls up on her pet cushion.

Kurt takes a sip, "Ahhhh, that's good." He sits back in the chair and closes his eyes.

I can see he needs a break, so I hold off asking him about the surgery.

When Kurt opens his eyes, he says, "Alice said you work downtown for an executive."

"Yeah, I do." I like that Kurt asked about me. Too many men I've dated don't seem interested in what I do to support myself.

"Do you like your job?"

"It's okay."

I do like my job even though I feel trapped there, but this is not something I want to talk about, so I change topics. "What do you do?"

"Night security at a mall. Sometimes I think about joining the police force though."

I want to stop talking about work-related issues and am curious about what happened at my neighbors. "How'd things go next door?"

"Mitch and Janet's friend was lucky. It was a small-caliber bullet that didn't go in deep, so it came out easy enough."

"How'd he get shot?"

Kurt takes a sip before answering. "That's not clear. From what I could gather, he might've sold some bad drugs and the man who got ripped off came after him."

"Janet said the man didn't want doctors and cops involved. Is that why you helped him?"

Kurt straightens up in his chair and takes a couple of deep gulps of the spiked tea before saying, "Friends help friends."

Kurt's reply, a simple truism, makes me wonder how Kurt knows John, Alice, Mitch, and Janet. Clearly, there's danger in the building around me, but I decide it's not so bad. The folks at the party tonight may have their problems, but they are a step up and away from the danger I always felt around Dad.

"Alice said you were a medic in the Army."

"Uh, . . . that's not quite right." Kurt looks out the window into the dark night before adding, "I flunked out of the Army's Medic School. But, before I got washed out of the program, I learned enough to be able to treat some gunshot wounds."

My mind goes over the evening, and I'm barely audible when I say, "I've never had a New Year's Eve like this one. I wonder what it means for the upcoming year."

Kurt's glance in my direction makes it clear he heard what I said. He reaches over and touches my arm. "I hope it means we'll get to know each other better in the new year."

His hand, the one that recently removed a drug-deal-gone-bad bullet, feels reassuring. I look at his face and imagine it holds secrets, secrets worse than my own, behind his kind eyes.

As Kurt clears his throat to say something, the phone interrupts with a harsh, intrusive tone. After a few rings, the answering machine kicks in and blares, "Where the fuck is everyone?" Then, a loud belch precedes the phone slamming down at the caller's end making a disconnect. Bean jumps up, and tension rises up my back into my shoulders.

Kurt asks, "Who or what was that?"

There's no way to avoid an explanation for the rude message other than telling the truth. "That's my alcoholic father. Mom left him two days after Christmas to live with her sister, and Dad doesn't know where she is. I don't want anything to do with him either." My lips and brow tighten as I fight back tears.

Kurt puts his drink down and pulls his chair around so that it's closer to mine. He leans in and puts his hands on my arms. "He sounds like a real asshole, Valerie."

I'm ashamed to look at Kurt and need time to get my thoughts off my family so I ask, "What's your family like?"

"Well, my father is a retired attorney and my mother, who died a few years ago, was an actress in local theater. Dad and I get along great, and we shared a condo until recently."

I think about my dad's job as a janitor. Kurt's family, so different from my own, makes me wonder what we have in common.

Kurt, whose hands are still on my arms, says, "Everything will be okay, Valerie. I'm on your side."

I look at him to make sure that he's being straight with me, and he is. I decide to follow up on our earlier conversation. "Kurt, you thought everyone at the party might be an outcast like in the Ginsberg poem. How are you an outsider?"

Kurt sits back and doesn't answer my question right away. It's his turn to look away from me. Then, he says, "Well, . . . I learned something about your family from your father's call, so. . ."

Kurt stops talking. When he looks my way, I watch his eyes move back and forth as he deliberates whether to go on. I wait to see if he'll continue, and he does.

"I don't usually tell anyone this no matter how long I've known them, but I'm adopted."

"Lots of people are adopted," is all I can think to say but hope it's reassuring.

"It's not being adopted that bothers me but how I learned about it."

Kurt goes silent, and I'm about to apologize for probing but Kurt continues, "When I was six, Mom got so mad at me that she blurted out, 'I wish we never adopted you.' I can't shake off being cast away, first from my birth mother and then cast off from the woman who adopted me."

"Geez, Kurt, I'm sorry. That's so much for a six-year-old to deal with."

"Yeah. Mom and I always had a rocky connection. It was different with my dad, though."

Our conversation revealed too many family secrets, so I lighten things by lifting my drink and saying, "Let's toast to the new year."

I smile and look into Kurt's eyes, eyes that sparkle at my own as we lean toward each other and tap drinks.

Kurt puts his cup down and asks, "Valerie, how 'bout going out on Saturday? You up for that?"

I nod. "Yeah."

"Do you enjoy adventures?"

"I do," is all I manage to say even though I'm wondering what he has in mind.

"Great. Can I pick you up around 7:00 in the morning?"

"Okay . . ." I say tentatively as I think, *Geez, that's early*.

Kurt chuckles and warns, "Dress warmly. I'll see you Saturday."

He gets up, grabs his leather jacket, and puts it on. I walk with him to the door where he gives me a hug and says, "Happy new year, Valerie."

I close my eyes and whisper into his ear, "You, too, Kurt."

He gives me a squeeze before releasing me and opening the door. I step into the hallway with him and watch as he heads down the stairs, pulling a knit hat and some gloves from his pocket. He begins whistling, and the pied-piper tune echoes up the stairwell causing a tingle to go through me.

I step back into my apartment, close the door, and go to the window where I follow Kurt's movement along snowy sidewalks to his car. He starts the engine and gets back out to chip ice off the windshield. After a few minutes, he stops, looks up to my apartment windows, and smiles when he sees me.

Ch. 6 - Fire and Ice

ONE HOUR BEFORE DAWN on a cold, January morning, I watch Kurt park his SUV on the street outside my apartment building. It's our first date, and I dash down the stairs arriving at the entryway door at the same time that Kurt comes up the sidewalk. I push open the door and join him outside.

"Morning." My voice is low so I won't disturb anyone this early on a Saturday.

"Morning, Valerie," Kurt whispers back, eyes glistening from the overhead streetlight. He appears to hold a secret that he's anxious to share. "I see you're ready for our adventure."

"I'm ready, but tell me something, Kurt." I put my hands on my hips, lower my eyelids, and cock my head to one side.

Concern replaces the delight I saw in his eyes a moment ago. "What?"

I relax my stance and smile. "Do all adventures begin before daylight?"

Kurt chuckles as he puts his gloved hand on my back, guides me to his SUV, and opens the door. "Some adventures do begin early, Valerie, some do."

I hop into his vehicle as he says, "We're in luck; it's not cloudy." Kurt's expression hints of some secret that he hasn't yet shared and one I can't puzzle out.

After he gets in the driver's seat, I ask, "Why's that important, having no clouds?"

"You'll see."

We travel deserted, predawn streets in his SUV. I'm curious about what he's so hepped up over this early on a cold morning.

"Where are we going?"

"You'll see that soon, too," Kurt says in a mysterious manner before pushing a CD into the player and humming along to the meditative tones.

I'm not sure what to say, so I sit back, relax, and enjoy Kurt's music as we drive along streets empty of other travelers. Before long, we enter a nature park where sunlight is beginning to filter through trees at the east side of the road. Kurt drives a couple of miles along the Chagrin River before pulling into a parking area near a trailhead.

He puts the car in park, steps out, opens the rear door, and grabs two backpacks from the rear seat. After I get out and come around to stand by his side, he says, "Here, take this one. It's lighter."

I heft the backpack on, and Kurt adjusts the straps to fit my frame. He swings the other backpack on, locks the vehicle, and looks me over. I've pulled the hood attached to my jacket up and over the knit hat I'm wearing.

"If you're cold, we don't have to do this, but the trail goes uphill from here. The exertion should warm us."

"Okay, I'm game."

We take a trail that climbs from the frozen riverbed, and I warm up enough from the effort to unzip my parka part way. There are no signs that others have walked here recently.

The crunch of our boots on frigid snow and our audible, labored breathing as we climb the steep hill are the only sounds in the dormant, winter woods. I look around and feel my soul awaken to a forest withdrawn into itself during this harsh season. Bare tree branches form a spidery web over our heads but light filters through. The days are getting longer, and there's an overriding sense that the dormancy will not last.

After a quarter-mile, the trail levels and follows a hollowed-out area in the shale. Sandstone overhangs the narrow path and forms a dark, gray roof. We walk another quarter mile until we reach a small grotto. Giant icicles dangle off the edge of the sandstone ceiling like medieval swords.

Kurt stops and crouches behind the icy daggers hanging at the front of the grotto, and I follow his lead. The sandstone is several feet over our heads while dark shale forms the curved back wall. We remove our backpacks, and Kurt takes a camera out of the bag he carried. "Wait for the sun to get a little higher," he whispers.

It feels right to speak softly within this winter sanctuary. "Why are we here?"

Kurt points to the bleak shale wall behind us where I see only a patchwork of small fissures in the dark rock. I look at Kurt and raise my shoulders and hands, a questioning expression on my face.

I barely hear Kurt say, "Wait."

A couple moments pass, and then ballroom-like shards of light burst upon the prehistoric stone behind us. I turn to face the rising sun and see ice glistening to life as it sparkles from the light. The sun's rays have pierced through the icicles hanging at the front of the grotto, and its impact is amazing.

Kurt gets busy capturing the magic of this fire on ice with his camera. I watch him move about, crouch in different places, change his angle of vision, and take photographs. He occasionally lowers his camera to study the scene before finding new angles from which to get a photo.

The magic ends when the sun rises too high to pierce through the icicles overhanging this icy cave. Kurt puts the lens cap back on his Canon and looks at me. The mystery I heard in his voice and saw in his eyes when he picked me up has been revealed, and I marvel at what this man knows.

He returns the camera to his backpack, winks at me, grabs the backpack I carried, and removes a thermos along with two coffee mugs. He hands me one of the cups, opens the thermos, and pours out hot chocolate. I let the steam from the warm beverage flow over my face.

"That was amazing. How often does this happen?"

"We lucked out, Valerie. If temperatures aren't right or icicles haven't formed or it's cloudy, this doesn't happen."

I sip the rich chocolate flavor in my mug and think about the sun's fire through ice. I point to Kurt's bag. "Are those cameras hard to use?"

"Not really. You can even set them on auto. Do you take pictures?"

"I've used point-and-shoot cameras but wondered about the type of camera you use. All the dials and numbers look complicated."

The sun is well above the horizon and throws bluish-white shadows from the trees onto the snow.

"This is a special place. How did you find it?"

"I didn't find it. My dad brought me here when I was a boy."

I take another sip of cocoa and enjoy the afterglow of bearing witness to one of nature's special moments.

Kurt continues, "Dad read a poem the first time he showed me this sunshine in ice."

"What poem?"

Kurt recites:

> Some say the world will end in fire,
> Some say in ice.
> From what I've tasted of desire
> I hold with those who favor fire.

Kurt's recitation triggers my memory of the poem by Robert Frost, and I add,

> But if it had to perish twice,
> I think I know enough of hate,
> To know that for destruction ice,
> Is also great . . .

Kurt joins me as I say the last line, "And would suffice."

Our high spirits, incompatible with the intensity of the apocalyptic poem, force us to laugh. Our eyes meet, and my breath goes quick and shallow under his gaze.

"Ready to pack up?" Kurt's still looking at me, and I feel a soul-to-soul connection to him.

We return everything to the backpacks and head back to the car. The steep descent to the parking area would have been icy if too many boots had packed down the snow, but with only our set of tracks laid out, it's a fast and secure downward footing.

We stow our backpacks, buckle into our seats, and pull out of the parking area. I remove my gloves and place my hands over the heating vents.

Kurt looks at me. "How 'bout something to warm you up at my place? Breakfast?"

"Grub sounds good."

"Grub?" Kurt laughs, and I join him. I'm not embarrassed by the word I used but happy to be able to let myself unwind with this man.

"Okay, Valerie, you got it. Grub coming up." Kurt looks my way and smiles as he drives north toward Lake Erie.

Twenty minutes later, Kurt pulls into a gated complex where two high-rise structures stand close to the shoreline. Kurt nods to security as the barrier lifts, drives past the guard, and parks in an underground facility. We gather up the backpacks and cross the dimly lit concrete to an elevator that takes us to the tenth floor. When we enter Kurt's condominium, he points to a door on the left. "You can hang your parka in there."

After stashing our outdoor gear in the closet, we go down a short hall and enter a spacious dining-living area. A counter with a flat-top stove separates the kitchen from the main area. A wall of windows from kitchen to dining area to living room features a view of the lake and distant downtown. Walls, couch, chairs, and kitchen cabinets in shades of white and cream intensify the natural light from the windows.

A cherry dining table and entertainment center offer a soothing contrast to the bright, airy atmosphere. There's an upright piano near the wall that separates the common area from what must be bedrooms and baths beyond. Accent tables made of glass have gunmetal gray supports that match the color of the granite counters and sleek cabinet pulls in the kitchen.

"Make yourself comfortable, Valerie, while I fix something to eat. Oh, the bathroom is down the hall past the piano."

This well-furnished condominium with its expansive view of the sky and Lake Erie smacks against the narrow circumstances of my working-class upbringing. I'm out of place and move about tentatively taking whisper-like breaths of air. If I inhale too much too quickly, I might spoil everything. I want to embrace Kurt and his world yet am subdued and shy.

While Kurt busies himself in the kitchen sautéing onion and green pepper for an omelet, I study the framed black-and-white photographs hanging over the piano. Many of them capture intriguing architectural lines on modern buildings. Others portray beautiful mountains in early morning mist. "Whose photos are these?"

Kurt looks up from whisking a half dozen eggs. "My dad's and mine. Dad lived here, too, before going to San Diego. Actually, this is his condo. Hey, Valerie, how about a mimosa?"

I'm not sure what that is but say, "Sure. Why not."

I watch Kurt pull a bottle of champagne from the wine refrigerator, pop it open, pour it into two tall glasses, and add orange juice. He whistles an upbeat, energetic tune as he works in the kitchen. His exuberance draws me in his direction, and I take a seat at one of the bar stools near the counter. "Who plays the piano?"

Kurt sprinkles cheese over the eggs in the skillet. "I do. Dad once thought private piano lessons would help me focus and get rid of nervous energy."

"Did it?"

Kurt laughs. "Dad would have been better off signing me up for football or sending me to mountaineering school. But I do love playing."

Kurt plates the omelet, retrieves some croissants that have been warming in the oven, and settles at the counter next to me.

"I love music, too," I tell Kurt. "If I hadn't cheated on an exam in sixth grade, though, I wouldn't have learned to read music or play an instrument."

"That's weird. What kind of test was it?"

"A test for musical abilities. I didn't know the answers, panicked, and copied from another student's exam. The person I cheated from did well because I got invited to take music lessons in middle school."

Kurt puts his fork down and drinks from his mimosa. "Geez, why didn't they just ask you if you wanted to learn music?"

"Yeah, really. That would have been better than swindling my way in."

"What did you play?"

"Trumpet. It's the instrument my dad preferred, but I wanted to play the piano."

I finish eating and watch Kurt brush crumbs from his hands. He asks, "Wanna learn some piano?"

"Now?"

"Sure, why not."

I'm reluctant, but Kurt takes my hand and leads me to the piano.

"I'd like to hear you play first if that's okay."

Kurt opens a music book, flips the cover off the keyboard, and plays "Here Comes the Sun" while humming along. I watch his fingers proceed through the piano keys until my eyes discover the blue bruises at the bend in his elbows. The marks remind me of what Alice said about Kurt, that he sometimes self-medicates with some strong stuff.

We sit close, so close that I feel the vibrations coming from his chest. He's either resonating with the piano or I feel the resonance from his body as he hums along to the tune he's playing. I shiver but am not sure whether it's an arousing tingle from being so close to him or a quick fear of Kurt's possible drug habit.

"That was lovely," I say when Kurt finishes playing.

"Your turn, Valerie."

I can't put off a lesson any longer. When he shows me where to position my hands on the keys to play a C major scale, my breathing gets short. I do my best to concentrate while attempting the scale and love it when Kurt says, "Well done."

Kurt puts his hands over mine to help me with three basic chords, C, F, and G. I feel the heat of his skin against mine. It feels right; it feels welcome.

After playing the chords and letting them sound out a few moments, I turn my head toward Kurt. He's looking at me and smooths some hair back from my face. My breath quickens when his hand caresses my neck. He moves closer, and his soft smile brushes my lips. My eyes close when his warm mouth meets mine, but it's a little too much, too soon, and I pull back. I can't help but glance at the icy, blue bruises visible at the edge of Kurt's rolled-up sleeves.

"Kurt, I had a great time and think I want to see you again."

"Think?" Kurt laughs, pushes his sleeves down, and covers up the marks on his arms. "Well, . . . okay." Kurt pauses a moment before adding, "Tell you what, call me if you want to go out next weekend. How's that sound?"

I look at him and nod. Kurt's take on life, whether with friends needing surgery or with capturing sunshine through ice or with mysterious marks on his arms, goes way beyond anything I've experienced. I need a little time and space away from him to make sure about my footing before I decide about crossing into his world.

Ch. 7 - Soul Searching

FOR SEVERAL DAYS AFTER my first date with Kurt, I think about calling him. Clearly, I'm attracted to him and, if I'm honest, I'm also intrigued by the side of him that he's keeping secret. I, too, carry secrets, not illegal ones like his might be, but harmful secrets nonetheless. On my part, I failed in my attempt to get the thing I wanted most in life – a college education.

Grades weren't the issue. I had no trouble maintaining top marks, but I didn't feel like I belonged among the students and professors. My inability to feel at home showed most clearly whenever I had to talk in class or give a presentation. My voice shook, and I couldn't breathe so I dropped out rather than face conversational French and the required speech class.

Now, I'm at a job that's no longer interesting. The work I did regarding the formation of a joint venture ceased when the taconite plant for which the partnership was formed began operation late last year. My workload tumbled from a hectic but challenging pace to a boring void. My boss's legal and financial expertise in shipping and mining is no longer called upon. The telephone rarely rings, and I do not need to coordinate travel, meeting, or luncheon venues. I'm at a loss about what to do with all the free time.

My boss wanders in and out of his office, and I know he, too, misses the excitement of being the head of an emerging partnership. At mid-week, he sits at his desk with a small vise, looks up, catches my gaze, and motions me in.

"It's a fly-tying kit."

Items arranged on his desk blotter look more like a sewing repair kit with scissors and thread, but in place of needles, I see sharp hooks.

"Oh, you're making your own fishing lures."

Also scattered on his desk are colorful "pipe-cleaner worms" and fuzzy shapes that I'm certain would intrigue Bean.

"I'm planning several fly-fishing trips in the near future," he tells me. "There wasn't much time to take a vacation over the past several years, and I'm looking forward to getting away more. So is my wife."

I return to my desk and think about Kurt. The needle-mark reason not to call him gets overruled by so many reasons to date him. I like that he served our country and knows about defending himself and the nation. He works security and has aspirations of becoming a police officer.

What intrigues me more, however, are the parts of him that cannot be measured in military rank or job title or income level. The magic of being out with him at dawn to see the sunrise glisten through icicles while crouched in a prehistoric cave and sharing the poetry of Frost captures my heart. The framed photographs on the wall of his home provide insight into how Kurt sees the world, and I'm enthralled with that vision. His musical abilities are sensitive and well-honed. His cooking isn't bad either.

I am at the end of personal options everywhere else in my life, but in the brief time I spent with Kurt, there are hints of doors to be opened and paths to be explored. I decide to call Kurt for a second date.

Ch. 8 - Windowpanes and Doorways

KURT ARRIVES AS I FINISH putting Saturday morning's breakfast dishes away. He has a black, nylon duffle with him that he sets on the couch before bending down to pet Bean.

"You asked about my camera last week. Wanna try using my dad's Nikon?"

I'm pleased that he listened when I asked about his camera during our first date. "Yeah, I'd love that."

"Good." He unzips the bag and hands me the Nikon. "Here, I'll help you get familiar with it."

Kurt moves behind me to guide my hands with his as he shows me how to hold the camera, how to switch it on with my thumb, and where to put my forefinger for the shutter release. I'm intrigued by these basic functions and practice autofocusing by pressing the button halfway before completing a few shots of Bean.

Kurt looks at the results in the viewfinder and says, "You catch on fast. I like that."

"Me, too."

"Grab a jacket, Valerie, and we'll head out."

"Do I need to dress for the tundra like I did last week?"

Kurt laughs. "No. We'll be indoors this time."

"Good."

"Actually, we'll be in a steamy jungle."

"Yeah, sure," I mumble as I grab a coat.

"You'll see, Valerie," Kurt says as we leave my place.

On the way down the stairs, we run into John who is sweeping the hallway. "Hey, Valerie."

"Hi, John."

John turns to Kurt, "I have something that might interest you."

Kurt looks at me, hesitates a moment, and then hands me the keys to his vehicle. "Let yourself in. I'll be there in a moment."

"Okay," I say before going outside to his SUV.

When Kurt gets in the driver's side a few minutes later, he says, "I have a membership to the botanical garden. We really will be in a jungle. There's a rain forest there. Have you been?"

The question preempts my intention to ask him about what John wanted. "No, but I've wanted to see it."

The Glasshouse, as the indoor greenhouse is called, opened at the garden center recently, but the ticket price is steep and out of my budget. It's a short drive during which I forget about John as I practice with the camera. Soon, we are driving past a concert hall and art museum as we approach the Glasshouse.

I lower the camera to look at the structure's support beams that launch upwards seemingly to probe the gray clouds. Crossbeams make an interconnected, web-like design around panes of glass that capture and reflect the snow-covered ground and the somber sky. It's a stunning piece of architecture that competes for attention with the silvery curves on a nearby building designed by Frank Gehry.

Kurt drives down a ramp to the Glasshouse's underground parking. From there, we ride an elevator to the main lobby, bypass the ticket counter, and gain quick admission using Kurt's membership card. Kurt tugs on my sleeve, "Let's go to the rainforest. It's my favorite section."

We go into a dimly lit vestibule separating the lobby from the jungle. When we open the second set of doors, the impact of a humid world is immediate and makes our lungs labor to pull in the dense, moisture-laden air. An indoor waterfall pounds down, splashes into a stream, and provides a constant drum-like beat as water splatters on concrete. Bird calls issue from dense greenery adding brassy high notes to the water's constant rhythm. I smell the rich, warm soil, a luscious scent that makes me want to plunge my fingers into the nurturing loam.

Kurt takes my hand. "Let's start on the canopy walk," he says. "We can get an overall view from up there."

We take the stairs to a raised walkway and look over a layer of thick, interwoven leaves that get disturbed occasionally by unseen creatures living within the greenery. Sometimes a bird hops into view, but at other times we cannot see whatever life form disturbed the leaves.

When we return to the main level, we walk to the waterfall where children splash and play in the small cave behind the water's tumbling shield. I watch Kurt put his Canon up to his eye and begin snapping a few photos. I raise the Nikon that Kurt loaned to me and look through the viewfinder, but I am uncertain where to focus my attention in the complex jungle around me.

When Kurt finishes and replaces the lens cap, I do the same. We walk along the stream and find a bench near the glass wall. A burst of sunlight escapes through winter clouds and warms my back as we sit down. The dewy moisture from the bench presses through my jeans, and I take a deep breath of the moist, rich air. "What a remarkable place."

Kurt looks at me. "What are you smiling about?"

"It feels good being here with you."

"So, you've made up your mind about me, then?"

In response to his question, I snuggle close, and he puts his arm along the bench behind me. I rest my head on his shoulder and take his free hand.

We make a quick tour of the desert side of the Glasshouse before driving to Kurt's place to view our photographs. As the images download from our cameras to a laptop, Kurt opens a bottle of wine. "Valerie, get a couple of glasses." He points to the cabinet over the wine refrigerator.

I get the wine glasses and pour while he puts some sandwiches together. I set a glass down near him, take a few quick swallows of the wine I poured for myself, and count on the alcohol to relax me. I'm still not feeling at home in the plush surroundings at Kurt's condo.

Once Kurt finishes in the kitchen, we sit side-by-side on the sofa to eat and view our images. There's a big difference between Kurt's photos, which delve into each subject, and mine, which skim surface themes. Kurt's photographs explore magnificently lined tree trunks and intricately patterned leaves. They highlight the velvety down on a giant moth wing, bring out the smooth detail in feathers on a bird, and capture the cottony flow of the indoor waterfall. In one image, a group of plants seems to swirl like ballerinas, and in another picture, stark architectural supports sparkle in the overhead glass.

Kurt's images of people are as artistic as his photos of plants, critters, and inanimate objects. Candid shots of children capture their eyes wide in wonder. In one photo, a child's elfish grin portrays a spirit seemingly conjured up from the dense jungle. Some photos depict more complex emotions. A man slouches forward with head in hands, some unseen weight pressing him down, while two young boys cavort joyfully nearby. Another image captures an elderly woman alone on a bench. Lost deep inside herself with age or sorrow, she sinks far away from the stunning beauty around her. Unaware of the many-layered jungle so close, it looks possible that she could be overrun by the foliage at any moment.

While viewing Kurt's photos, it dawns on me how much I didn't see while I was in the Glasshouse. I do not like discovering this part of myself that seems shut off from and blind to my surroundings. I get up and move across the room to the windows so Kurt won't see me struggle to understand how blind I feel.

After a moment, Kurt shuts down the computer, gets up, and stands behind me. "Is everything okay?"

I can't face him but manage to whisper, "I stood right there next to you and didn't see any of what you caught in your photos." I fight back tears and have trouble speaking. "I wonder how much of the world I miss seeing all the time even when it's right in front of me."

"Are you seeing more now?"

I look at the view from Kurt's condominium and see clouds highlighted by the moon's glow over an icy lake. In the distance, there's a gray silhouette of the city's skyline lit up against the night sky. "You know, I *am* beginning to take in more of what I see."

"That's what matters, Valerie. Besides, too many people live lives of desperation rather than open up to the marvels around them, and I don't think you're one of those people."

Kurt refers to a line I admire from Henry David Thoreau's *Walden*, about how many people live "lives of quiet desperation." I'm not sure that my circumstances mean I'm *not* quietly desperate, but I get hopeful when Kurt says that he doesn't think I am caught in such a life.

"You know, your photos are artfully composed. Many people can't frame a scene as well as you do." My face brightens from the encouragement. Kurt's kindness, so unfamiliar, almost hurts though. The pleasure I experience being with Kurt intertwines with fear of the unfamiliar to create a bittersweet mixture that puts me off balance.

My internal struggle must show because Kurt asks, "Valerie, are you okay?"

"Kurt, I'm a bit overwhelmed."

"Do you want to go home?"

"No. You've shown me so much that I've never seen or experienced before. That's all. I'm being silly."

"You aren't silly, Valerie."

Kurt puts his arm around me, and I lean into him. He takes a breath and then hesitates as if he had changed his mind about saying something. "What? What were you going to say?"

After a moment, he says, "Valerie, remember when John stopped me earlier?"

"Yeah, what was that about?"

"He gave me something that might be fun and relaxing. Wanna try a light hit of acid?"

LSD, touted as one of the creative influences behind some of the music from the 1960s, was taken by Aldous Huxley who not only wrote *Brave New World* but also penned *Doors of Perception*, based on his experience taking mescaline. Could LSD open a door for me?

"I'd like to try it."

"Have you ever dropped LSD?"

I shake my head.

"John says one gel tab is a light dose."

Kurt tears off a small piece of translucent gel that he calls a windowpane and hands it to me. "Chew on it a bit before swallowing."

I place it in my mouth and watch Kurt take a similar-sized dose.

"It could take 30 minutes to an hour to feel anything," he says as he tunes in a jazz station on the FM receiver. The music is soothing, an interplay of piano, double bass, and drum.

Kurt leads me back to the couch, refills my wine glass, and retrieves a book on photography before settling down next to me. He opens the hardcover volume, explains how to highlight a foreground subject against a blurred, out-of-focus background, and points out some principles of composition. I'm learning about some of the camera's depth-of-field controls, thinking about how to frame subject matter, and enjoying the lesson. As Kurt turns another page of the large, glossy manual, I see a blurry trail follow his arm. The colors in the photographs on the newly opened page appear to pulse and vibrate.

The book rests across our laps, our thighs aligned one against the other, and all my senses flow toward Kurt. I look at his face and see eyes sparkling with a light so deep that the secrets of the universe seem to reside there almost within reach. Kurt's fingers trace my palm and send exhilarating currents up my arm.

He gets up and beckons me to join him. A gentle piano riff opens "In A Sentimental Mood," and I reach out for Kurt. As our hands join, I hear a saxophone slide into the mix coming from the speakers. Kurt hugs me from behind, his chin resting on my shoulder, his hands caressing my belly. The warmth of his palms on my tummy radiates throughout my body.

Aroused, I turn to face him as the next tune begins with a sexy saxophone that whines, teases, pleads, and urges during "Dancing in The Dark." Brassy tonal licks penetrate from ear to libido, and I yearn to answer the feral calls I hear in the music. Kurt nestles his cheek in my hair, and we sway to the tune as a piano joins the sax in lovely improvisation.

We slow dance with our bodies pressed close together, and I blend into Kurt and the jazz tones until I feel like I've become one with him and the music. I want the excitement of my bare skin on Kurt's, so I lean back from him and unbutton his shirt. My hands slide across his shoulders and down his arms as I move the shirt off his body. I remove my blouse and savor the touch of my breasts on Kurt's chest.

My hands fondle the back of Kurt's neck. His hands take my buttocks and press me to him. He hardens as his lips travel down to tease my nipples. A moaning sound escapes my throat. We're breathing hard and there's no question that we want each other. Kurt guides me down the hall to the bedroom where soft lighting above a shelf near the ceiling provides a subtle glow. Speakers next to a bureau continue the jazz from the living room in a seamless sea of sound. We throw off jeans and underwear and sink onto the bed's comforter.

Kurt's lips move down my throat, between my breasts, and settle on my belly. When his lips return to mine, I wrap my legs around his waist and pull him toward me. We are two instruments of flesh that hunger for each other. Skin-on-skin sizzles out an improvisation between us, and I pull him closer into a crescendo of orgasms.

Satiated sexually and coming down from the acid, we rest with arms and legs intertwined. Out of the bedroom window, I can see the lights from the distant city go out in anticipation of a new day. We've been up all night, and our appetites shift from sexual pleasure to a desire for breakfast. I slip into one of Kurt's oversized flannel shirts while Kurt puts on a pair of jeans.

We decide on mimosas, croissants, and an omelet to repeat the menu we had for breakfast one week ago on our first date. This time, though, I'm in the kitchen by Kurt's side as we prepare the meal. In Kurt's presence and the drug's afterglow, I am more sensually awake and profoundly happy than I've ever been.

Ch. 9 - Entering the Ring

KURT ASKS ME TO spend the weekends at his place. I know that it's easier to say "no" at first rather than jump in the ring with a "yes" only to find I'm outmatched when the bell sounds and the round begins. Although Kurt claims that the bruising on his arms resulted from giving a lot of blood in the military, I'm skeptical. Alice had warned me on New Year's Eve that Kurt may be losing control of his painkillers. I need to understand what I may be getting into if Kurt and I get closer, so I visit Alice one evening after work. John lets me in and tells me Alice is making lasagna.

I follow the aroma of a basil-infused tomato sauce as I walk to the kitchen. "Hey, Alice. Boy, something smells good."

"Hey, Val. How are you and the calico doing?"

"I've named her Bean, and we're fine."

"Good to hear."

Alice puts pasta noodles into boiling water, looks at my troubled face, and says, "You must have something on your mind. What's up?"

"Well, Kurt and I began seeing each other after your New Year's Eve party."

"I thought so. John said he saw you two going out last weekend." As she spreads sauce onto a baking dish, she asks, "Is everything okay?"

"Yeah, I'm having a good time."

"So, what's up?"

"I'm not sure how to ask this."

Alice looks up from the noodle she's testing for tenderness. "Val, spit it out."

"Okay." I take a deep breath not sure I want to know more about Kurt's drug use. "Um . . . at the party, you said Kurt used some heavy stuff, and I saw some bruising on the inside of his elbows."

Alice pauses a moment before turning off a burner and draining the noodles.

"Val, help me layer this pasta dish. Once it's in the oven, we'll talk."

What I learn from Alice about Kurt's drug use does not stop me from spending weekends at his condo. Sure, he has problems, maybe big problems. Due to having an alcoholic father, I'm familiar with troubled men and am not put off by Kurt because Kurt has shown me how magical life can be. Kurt's take on life is expansive rather than mean as my father's life had been.

I wanted a better place in the world ever since getting into advanced placement classes starting in second grade. There, I learned a wider view than the one I knew from my working-class family, but I had no idea how to bridge the social-class gap between me and students from better circumstances.

The gap was so large that by the time I arrived in high school, I knew my place and concentrated on office management courses like bookkeeping and computer spreadsheets rather than take college prep. When I became administrative assistant to an executive, the personnel manager pointed out my poor grammar in an attempt to dissuade my boss from hiring me. That criticism from the personnel department prompted me to listen to my speech, and I heard my family's "you'uns," often shortened to "yinz" (plural for you), and my inherited mismatch of some verbs with their subjects. Mom and Dad always said "they was" and "we was." It took a while for my tongue to speak the correct forms because they felt rocky rough coming out of my mouth.

Who am I, a woman with an alcoholic father from a working-class family, to shun anyone because of bluish bruises on their arms?

I begin living with Kurt on weekends, and the experience provides access to a world where people eat better food, wear nicer clothes, have plusher furnishings, live in upscale neighborhoods, and drive luxury cars. It is a world where vegetables do not come from cans and where bread has crust so firm, a person can almost stand on it.

Most weekends, we stay indoors away from a wind that sends cold gusts across Lake Erie. One of my favorite pastimes during our winter weekends is working through music books on Kurt's piano. I watch his playing, emulate his piano technique, and learn to create an expressive connection from my soul to the sounds I produce. Kurt notices the change I make in my playing ability as I work out the first few bars of Chopin's Prelude in E-Minor one weekend in February.

"Whoa, Valerie, that's lovely. The emotional expression is wonderful."

I look at him to make sure he isn't teasing me and find his face sincere.

"My piano instructor described that type of playing as the ability to free notes caught on the musical staff so that they soar into the heavens. It took me a long time to learn to play like that, and you're doing it already. Well done, Val."

My jaw drops, and I stare at him as if he materialized genie-like.

"What? What's wrong?"

"I'm not used to being with someone who enjoys this type of music and knows how to appreciate it. Whenever I tuned in the classical station at home to hear Mozart or Debussy, my parents called it funeral music. I thought you were messing with me."

Kurt asks, "Was I wrong to say something?"

"No . . . NO!" My emphasis underscores my need to let the kudos from Kurt, like long overdue rain, sink in. Kurt, who stands behind the piano bench, puts his arms around me and I lay my head back against his chest. His drug habits are of no concern to me.

Ch. 10 - From Hoar Frost to Desert Storm

ON A FRIGID SATURDAY MORNING, Kurt shakes me while I'm sleeping, "Valerie, get up!"

I stir. "Hmm . . . what?"

"Come on. Wake up." Kurt shakes me again. "You don't want to miss this."

"Miss what?" I sit up and watch Kurt scramble into some warm clothes. "What's going on?"

"You'll see," he says as he tosses my clothes on the bed.

"This better be good, Kurt." I'm sleepy and want to stay under the warm comforter.

Kurt grabs our cameras while I get up and dress. "Fog rolled in off the lake during the night."

"So?"

"In this cold weather, fog makes a special type of frost. Come on, Val."

I shake off my slumber and pull on boots, parka, hat, and gloves. Kurt hands me my camera, and we leave for the building elevator. No one else is about on the ground floor this early, not even the building's personnel.

Outside, we walk the wooded area east of the high-rise as the sun's light begins to show over the horizon. The trees are covered in numerous, white crystals that make their branches bow down over the trail to form a white tunnel around us. The fog and cold had covered everything with tiny, needle-like spires.

My breath is visible in the air. "What is this?"

"It's called hoar frost."

"Whore, like prostitute?"

Kurt laughs sending his breath into the air as visible clouds. "No, not prostitution. The word is spelled differently and comes from an Old English term meaning 'like an old man's beard'."

The lovely crystallized structures look more like miniature church steeples than a beard to me. My camera skills have improved, and I know what I want to capture and how to do it. When the morning sun disperses the fog, the edges of the crystalline formations blaze in sharp contours and shapes. It's the golden hour after dawn, one of the best times during the day for photography and for feeling alive.

The next night, I'm the one who wakes Kurt in the early morning when I slide out of bed to use the bathroom. I'm hungover from the wine we drank during the day and stumble into the nightstand next to the bed making a small, metal lamp wobble into a tap-dancing sound. Before I can catch the lamp, it crashes onto the granite-topped table. The noise sends Kurt leaping out of bed. There's enough moonlight coming in the window for me to see Kurt looking dazed, even hypnotized, like he's sleepwalking. I don't think he's sleepwalking, though, because his hands go up to grab me. His intent seems sinister, and I duck in time to avoid his reach. His hands smack into the wall instead of into me, and he stops moving.

I run to the doorway and flick on the overhead light. The bright beam from above makes Kurt blink and shake his head. He seems puzzled as he stands with his face to the wall. I'm not sure he realizes that I'm there with him. When I see him look around the room with eyes able to focus on reality, I whisper "Kurt."

He turns his head in my direction.

"Valerie?"

"Kurt, what happened?"

"I'm not sure. You tell me."

"You leaped up when I knocked over a lamp."

Kurt looks puzzled as he says, "I heard something detonate outside my barracks, or . . . or, I dreamed about a bombing." Kurt appears more alert when he adds, "I . . . I thought I was back in Iraq. Did I hurt you?"

"No, I'm fine."

It's 3:00 a.m., and Kurt looks troubled but doesn't want to talk.

"Valerie, go back to bed and get some sleep."

"Are you okay, Kurt?"

"Yeah, but I need some time alone."

"What can I do?"

"Leave me alone for a while." His voice is sharp, so I back down.

"Sorry. Look, I'm going to read until I settle down. Okay?"

Kurt walks away from me and goes down the hall to the living room where I hear him plop down on the couch. Kurt doesn't turn on any lights, so I know he's not reading. I lie in bed shaken by what happened and by Kurt's brusque dismissal of me. I'm a bit scared of how fast he came at me and fear what might have happened if I hadn't gotten out of his way in time. I don't get out of bed to approach him until I smell coffee brewing a few hours later.

"Morning, Kurt."

"Coffee?"

"Sure."

Kurt pours me a cup but seems hard and distant. He doesn't bring up what happened during the night and his demeanor indicates not to ask him about it. Anyway, I haven't shared the darker parts of my own life with him so why should I probe into his?

Ch. 11 - Death by Hypothermia

"VALERIE DEAR, I'M AFRAID there's bad news." It is mom's sister calling from West Virginia.

I sit down. "Aunt Cora, is Mom okay?" I look over to Kurt who just drove me home after spending Friday and Saturday nights at his place. He's letting Bean out of her carrier.

"She's fine, dear. It's your dad."

I brace myself for the news.

"Your father died."

"What?"

"He was found lying in the backyard this morning."

"What happened?"

"Oh, Valerie, this isn't easy to say."

"What isn't?"

"Your father froze to death. The coroner ruled it death by hypothermia. There was no evidence of foul play. According to the owner of the neighborhood bar, your dad staggered out around 1:00 a.m. Police interviewed the neighbor who saw your father lying in the snow at 6:00 a.m. and called 911. I am so sorry to tell you this, Valerie."

I don't know what to say and look at Kurt who raises a questioning brow as he watches me.

"Valerie, are you there?"

"Yes . . . yes."

"Are you okay enough to handle an obituary for the newspaper? Your mother isn't up to it."

I put my hand over the receiver and whisper to Kurt, "Dad died."

When I return my attention to Aunt Cora, I tell her, "I'll do the obit."

"Good."

"Can I talk with Mom?"

"She's not ready to talk right now. She's kind of feeling numb with the news about Paul and the need to deal with the cremation arrangements."

"Is there anything else I can do?"

"I can't think of anything. We'll be in town tomorrow. Talk then, okay?"

I'm a little numb myself and forget to hang up the phone, so Kurt takes the receiver from my hand and replaces it on its cradle.

The man who treated me with hatred is gone. The man who stirred up my hatred for him is dead. The man who made me violate the commandment about honoring your father passed away. I'm not feeling the grief I'm supposed to feel as his daughter. It seems there's nothing to grieve because Dad never made a positive connection with me, and I don't feel any loss.

Kurt asks, "Valerie, are you okay?"

"Yeah, I am. I'm tired I guess."

Kurt hugs me, pats my back, and whispers, "It's okay, Valerie."

Kurt calls in sick rather than work his night shift, and we lie down together. He strokes my hair and says, "It's okay, Val. I'm here." And, it is okay. Bean jumps up and nestles close. It's peaceful with the warmth of Kurt on one side and my cat on the other. Is it possible that my father can no longer hurt me? Am I really free from Dad and what he did to me?

When I write the obituary, I leave out the word "loving" as in "loving wife, Ruth Ann, and daughter, Valerie."

> Paul Willis, 51, formerly of Cedar Grove, West Virginia, died February 10, 2002, in Cleveland, Ohio. Born April 2, 1950, son of the late John and Mary Willis. He is survived by his wife, Ruth Ann, and daughter, Valerie. Paul served in the Vietnam War. Cremation is February 13. Family and friends will gather for a memorial service on February 28 at the VA cemetery in Grafton, WV. In lieu of flowers, donations may be made to the veterans' organization Operation Second Chance.

Ch. 12 - A Good Hit

KURT GOES WITH ME TO THE CREMATORY where he meets my mom, aunt, and uncle. Mom is too distraught and preoccupied to acknowledge Kurt's condolences. She spends what little energy she has signing papers and trying to understand what she must do in the coming weeks. With her husband's death and probate on her mind, she has little inclination to meet my new boyfriend.

Aunt Cora had warned me that Mom was withdrawn, and she's right. Mom's vacant eyes and distant demeanor are spooky. She manages to give a signal for Uncle Pete to begin the process by pushing a button that sends Dad's cremation casket into the furnace. As Father's remains pass by, I say "Goodbye" and Uncle Pete salutes.

Aunt Cora invites me and Kurt to go back to the house where I grew up. She and Uncle Pete put together a small buffet and think my being there to support Mom is a good idea. I agree to go although I'm not sure about returning to the house where I used a pepper-based spray against Dad the last time I was there. For Mom, this is the first time she has been in that house in over two months.

Kurt and I pull into the driveway behind Uncle Pete's car. February days are short, and it's already dark and cold. We all stand a moment on the back porch to stomp snow off our shoes before entering the house. Although Aunt Cora and Uncle Pete did their best to remove the debris left by Dad (crumpled newspapers, overflowing ashtrays, empty beer cans, and liquor bottles), the stale smell lingers.

We are surprised when Mom sits in Dad's favorite chair, a piece of furniture we thought she would avoid. She startles us when she begins mumbling, and we can't understand what she's saying. Rather than set out food, we sit near Mom to comfort her and show support. Her incoherent speech continues for several minutes while her eyes stare into a distant place. At a moment when we think there's no way to reach Mom, her words harden to cut clean and clear from her throat.

"I shouldn't have left him. He'd still be alive if I hadn't." Tears form in her eyes, eyes now sharply focused on blame. "I killed him."

Aunt Cora crouches next to Mom and takes her hand. "You didn't kill him, sweetie."

Mom closes her eyes.

I move close to her and whisper, "Everything will be okay, Mom."

Her eyes pop open, and she glares at me. "You fought with him and sprayed him with a nasty chemical on Christmas Eve! We both killed him."

I'm horrified by her accusation and back away. A sour taste comes up my throat as I wonder, *did my anger help kill Dad?*

Mom leaps up, which scares me since I've never seen her erupt before. Her eyes focus on me as she shouts, "Get out of here!"

My mouth drops open, and my heart races. I'm beginning to feel guilty for my role in Dad's death, and I stare at Mom, my accuser.

Aunt Cora takes me by the shoulders. "Valerie, look at me!"

I turn my head from my mother to my aunt.

"Valerie, your mom doesn't mean what she's saying. She's mad at herself, and some of her irritation is getting directed at others. She's already accused me and Pete of taking her away from your dad, and now she's taking her anger out on you."

Aunt Cora puts her hand on my back and guides me to the kitchen, away from Mom, while Uncle Pete settles my mother on the couch.

"I don't understand why she is so upset. Dad treated her like shit."

"Her behavior is hard to understand. Pete thinks she suffers from the Stockholm syndrome in which a person identifies with the tormentor."

Mom fumes in the background and struggles to get free of Uncle Pete who has his arm wrapped around her shoulder. Aunt Cora tells Kurt it's best if he takes me home, so he helps me into my coat and leads me out the door.

The drive back to my place is a blurred trace of a memory. I sit stunned, not by Dad's death but by Mom's accusation. It may be true that

I played a role in Dad's death. Kurt tries to console me, but I do not pay attention to what he says.

Somehow, I become aware of being in my own apartment. I don't remember the walk from Kurt's car up the stairs, and I don't remember unlocking the door.

I'm relieved to be in my own place and sitting on my own couch with Kurt, his arm around my shoulder.

"I thought that when I was free of that awful man, I'd be completely happy. I thought Mom would be happy, too. Now everything has turned upside down, and I feel guilty. What went wrong? I'm not sure I can deal with the thought that I may have played a role in Dad's death."

"Valerie, I know what it's like to think that you've played a role in another person's death. After the war, I brought home the knowledge that I killed people."

"How do you deal with it? I'm not sure I'll ever feel better."

Kurt reaches into a pocket and pulls out a small leather case, unzips it, and removes a tiny baggie with powder in it. "I have something that could help."

I've enjoyed the weed Alice gave me during the holidays and liked the acid I dropped with Kurt a month ago. I don't see any reason not to try a powder.

"You know what? I can sure use something stronger than alcohol or weed."

"Okay." Kurt opens the baggie, takes out a small mirror, and sprinkles some powder onto the mirror. He removes a razor from his kit and uses it to separate the powder into a few lines before rolling up a crisp dollar bill and handing it to me.

"How do I do this?"

Kurt retrieves the rolled-up tube and demonstrates how to snort drugs. I watch him inhale a line. "Don't breathe out as you lean in."

It's my turn. I place the tube in one nostril, close off the other one with a finger, breathe out, lean in, and do what Kurt showed me.

"Good hit," he says.

A few moments later, I sink back onto the sofa cushions, rest my head on Kurt's shoulder, and love the feeling of not having a care in the world.

Ch. 13 - A Predatory Inheritance

MOM'S ANGER TURNED into an eerie silence by the time I see her in Cedar Grove, West Virginia. She traveled there with her sister after Dad's cremation. I drive the car I inherited, and arrive on the morning of Dad's memorial.

We are in Uncle Pete's car for the drive to the VA cemetery in Grafton, about 100 miles away. Mom, who refuses to speak to anyone, sits next to me in the back seat. Dad's urn rests on her lap and creates a strange fifth presence in the vehicle.

Mom and I face away from each other, and I study the cloudlike fog rising from the West Virginia hills. It's the end of February, windy and cold. Gray skies hover over barren trees, and pockets of snow linger in the hollows between mountain ridges. Uncle Pete comments about the kindnesses of several of my father's childhood friends and some veteran buddies who are following us to the memorial service. Mainly, we take Mom's cue that she doesn't want to talk and remain silent.

When we arrive at the cemetery, a VA representative takes the urn from Mom while another representative organizes and escorts our small caravan of cars to the committal shelter. Dad's remains are placed near a partially folded American flag. Kurt, who couldn't get time off to be present, sent flowers. He also made a donation in Dad's name to Operation Second Chance, and his acknowledgment card rests among several other similar cards. After everyone takes a seat, Uncle Pete goes to the front and gives a brief eulogy.

"I often heard a poem, called The Soldiers Prayer, that speaks about a soldier who meets Saint Peter at the gates of heaven. The soldier knows he's in the right place because he had already served his time in hell when he was at war."

The veterans nod and mumble agreement with the sentiment while some of the women say, "Amen to that, brother."

Uncle Pete salutes Dad's ashes and the American flag. "Rest in peace, soldier."

After Pete returns to his seat, two military personnel lift the American flag from the table. With clean, precise movements, their white-gloved hands fold the flag and respectfully present it to Mom as taps plays in the background. The Honor Detail's drawn-out salute captures the solemnity of the occasion and the respect everyone has for this veteran. We stand and pass by Dad's urn to give our last farewell.

On the return trip to Cedar Grove, Mom and I are separated in the backseat by the folded American flag in its triangular memorial case. Her lap, now vacant of Dad's remains, seems impossibly empty, an emptiness I see in her eyes. Her blank stare scares me, so I keep my face turned away from her.

Aunt Cora comments on the service, "The VA did a very nice memorial for Paul."

Mom doesn't respond to the comment, and no one finds anything to say that might dispel Mom's icy presence. Uncle Pete tunes in a classical station, and the haunting notes to "The Lark Ascending," a composition by Vaughan Williams, create a meditative atmosphere. The music undergirds our inability to find the words that would reach Mom, heal her withdrawal from us, and overcome the distance that her silence produces.

When we arrive at Wakem's bar to meet the others who attended Dad's service, it's a relief to get out of the car and away from Mom. Wakem's warm atmosphere and cold drink allow words unspoken at the public ceremony to flow freely among friends in private.

Mom sits in a corner booth with her sister and nods at those who stop by with their condolences, but she doesn't say anything. I keep my distance and take refuge from her chilly countenance by drinking a beer and a shot of whiskey.

Uncle Pete knew my father fairly well, so I grab another beer and walk over to the barstool where he sits.

"Hey, Uncle Pete. Nice sentiment for Dad, the one about serving time in hell as a soldier."

Uncle Pete gives me a hug. "I thought it was appropriate for Paul.

"Dad's time in Vietnam was always a mystery to me. Do you know anything about it?"

"Not much. Your father rarely talked about his time there." Uncle Pete takes a sip from his beer. "He did, though, obsess over an experience he had only 12 days after arriving."

"What happened?"

"Why don't we find a table where we can talk privately." We leave the bar and settle into a booth.

"Let's see," Uncle Pete says as he rubs his chin. "Your dad arrived in Vietnam with another 20-year-old recruit named Nick. He and Nick joined a convoy of replacement soldiers heading to a place called Dak To when they were ambushed, and Nick got shot in the head. He and your father had switched seats during the journey, and your dad always thought the bullet should have killed him instead of Nick."

"How did you know that about Dad?"

"Paul came home with a drug problem and, as he got over it, he kept repeating the story about Nick. It must have haunted him more than any other thing that happened there, but he quit talking about Nick and Vietnam when he married your mom."

I sit back from the table and think about what Uncle Pete said. It's new information about my father, and I'm very curious about what kind of drug problem Dad had. "Can you tell me about Dad's drug use?"

Pete lets out a long sigh. "I guess you have a right to know. Look, some soldiers used drugs, including heroin, in Vietnam, and your dad was one of them."

"Geez, Uncle Pete, did Dad use heroin when he got home?"

"Thankfully, no."

"What happened? Was he in treatment?"

"From what I understand, once your dad returned home, he found it difficult to buy drugs in our little backwoods town. Plus, being out of intense, daily combat, eliminated his need for heroin."

"He quit without treatment? That seems impossible."

"Yeah, it puzzled me for a long time. Then, I volunteered at a veterans' hospital where I learned that many Vietnam veterans who used narcotics overseas could quit without treatment once they were home. It had something to do with a lack of access to narcotics, the elimination of warlike stressors, and personal factors like solid social support from family. Your mom was a big factor in your dad's case because he wanted to be free of drugs for her."

"But, alcohol's a drug, and Dad drank a lot."

Uncle Pete lets out a long breath of air. "Yeah, and losing the beer joint started his drinking problem."

"What beer joint?"

"Oh, I thought you knew." Pete takes a swig of his beer, thinks a bit, and adds, "About a year after his discharge from the military, your dad and a couple of friends went in together to buy a drinking establishment. They named it the Wonder Bar. For a while, your father thrived because he was one of the bosses and felt like what he called a 'kingpin'."

"What happened to the bar?"

"No one knows for sure, but we think your dad and the other co-owners didn't have the background to run a small business. They may not have done all the necessary paperwork or filed taxes properly. Who knows? After they built up a steady group of customers, the bank stepped in and foreclosed. That's when your father began drinking heavily."

There's so much to take in. I've lived with Dad for over 20 years and only now, after his death, am beginning to know him. I lower my eyes and think about my father in a new light, one that shakes up my sense of who I am and who he was.

Uncle Pete misinterprets my silence as unhappiness about what I learned. "Maybe I shouldn't have told you all that."

"Uncle Pete, no, I'm glad you did. This helps me a lot. I'm beginning to understand why Dad acted the way he did, but it's a lot to take in and process."

"I bet it is. I'm sure the information helps you understand him, but it doesn't excuse what he put you and your mother through."

No, it doesn't. I'm glad that Uncle Pete is being straight with me. He knows that having facts is important and doesn't fall back on the worn adage about not speaking ill of the dead. I'm glad that he's willing to speak frankly because the truth helps me get through what he knows was a difficult upbringing.

Uncle Pete closes his eyes, lowers his head, and exhales. He looks as if he's trying to decide whether or not to continue. When he opens his eyes and looks at me, he says, "There's something else about Vietnam and Nick's death. Although your father quit talking about surviving when Nick didn't, your mom said she could always sense Nick's presence in the house."

"But," Pete goes on, "your father worked hard and went to his job every day even though he hated cleaning toilets, dealing with other people's garbage, and scrubbing floors in that office building. He stayed there because the job was steady and paid well, and he always went home to give your mother his paycheck."

I turn my face away from my uncle and take a few swigs of beer as I reflect about what I learned. It reminds me of my own drug use and how much I feel trapped at my job like Dad must have felt trapped in his. There's a slow yet insistent turn of mental synapses in my brain that pushes an unsettling question into awareness: *Am I more like my father than I thought?*

Uncle Pete speaks and brings me back to our conversation. "Yes, your family had problems, but your dad made sure you had a roof over your head and food on the table."

I let the statement go since, as a child, I knew from kids who lived in the local children's home that the state would have done that much if I'd been an orphan.

Aunt Cora motions for Uncle Pete to join her near Mom. "Looks like I'm needed elsewhere," Uncle Pete says, "but, if you want to know more about your father, go talk to the man at the end of the bar. His name is Leonard Andinore, and his family lived next door to your dad when they were children. He can tell you about your father as a kid."

"Thanks, Uncle Pete." I give him a big hug, pick up my beer, and walk over to a man with curly hair, a wiry mustache, and a very lined face.

"Hi, . . . uh . . . Mr. Andinore?

"Yes?" He turns to look at me. "You're Paulie's kid, Valerie, ain't you?"

"Yeah, I am."

"Well, nice to meet ya." We shake hands. "Call me Lenny. How are you and your mom doing?"

"We're fine, I guess. Well, I am but Mom's taking it hard."

"She'll be okay. It'll take some time, but she'll be fine. What can I do for you?"

"Uncle Pete tells me you knew my dad as a child."

"I did."

"What was he like back then?"

"Hmm," Lenny pauses and stares down at his drink. "My mom and pop worried about him as a kid."

"Why?"

When Lenny looks up, he doesn't meet my eyes. "His mom, your grandmother, blew up a lot at Paulie. He'd come to our place after one of her rants feelin' all mad and then pick a fight with me. Pop said Paulie acted out because he was mad at his ma and worked it out by fighting with other kids."

Lenny's comments make me realize that my dad's temper stems from his own childhood abuse. It doesn't excuse how he treated me and Mom, but it helps explain it in a way that means his anger wasn't caused by me. I always thought I was too bad or too undeserving to be loved by him.

Lenny looks up at me as he realizes something about Dad's family. "You know, on top of it all, Paulie's dad favored the oldest boy."

"You mean my Uncle Ed?"

"Yeah. Nothin' your pa did was ever good enough compared to Ed."

I don't know my Uncle Ed because Dad and he parted ways decades ago. He lives somewhere in New York City and doesn't know about Dad's death because we have no contact information for him. I pick up a pitcher of beer, refill my glass, and say, "Dad was very hard to live with."

"I'm not surprised, Valerie. Your pop ended up with a big chip on his shoulder, and no one could get through his anger to help him. My parents tried, but . . ." Lenny throws up his hands in a helpless gesture.

Lenny puts a comforting arm along my shoulder. "Valerie, your pa seemed like a walkin' bomb with a short, always lit, fuse. I dislike myself for this, but I was relieved when he moved away 'cuz I had little kids by then, and his rantings scared 'em."

Those rantings certainly scared me.

This new knowledge about Dad's abusive, angry childhood invades my mind with a predatory force. It adds to the discomfort I feel over how much I may be like my father. Will I mimic Dad's violence when I have a family? What terrible, personal inheritance might I have received from Dad?

I decide I'd better leave before I drink too much and say things I shouldn't, so I turn to Mr. Andinore. "Lenny, thanks for telling me about my dad. It helps me more than you know to understand who Dad was as a child."

"Valerie, if you or your ma need anything, call on me. Okay?"

It's a lot to take in, and I want to be alone so I head for the door without saying anything to Mom. I catch Aunt Cora's eye and wave goodbye as I go out.

The lively country music inside Wakem's bar turns into a quiet thudding bass when the door closes. Street lamps and security lights from a few storefronts replace the subtle barroom lighting as I walk down Cedar Grove's short business district. It's Thursday, a weeknight, and the small-town tranquility gets disturbed only when a car passes by, which isn't often. I turn onto a street where no lights glow from inside the homes. Empty-looking house windows, shades pulled, reflect porch lights in this neighborhood where residents have retired for the day. Those reflected spots of light in the windows look like predatory animal eyes. I avert my gaze and hurry past.

The paved street and sidewalk end after a few blocks, and I walk my aunt and uncle's rural road. There's a mile to go, and it's dark. I can barely see the road and must follow a dim outline of light laid out on the lane between rows of towering trees. I learned to navigate a moonless night this way as a teen on the rare occasions when my family visited Mom's sister. It's scary yet thrilling to travel more by intuition than clear sight.

I hadn't noticed a breeze while in town but now hear it pushing through dead-looking branches making admonishing clacks. Old childhood fears about ghosts and other apparitions send a prickle up my spine and into my hairline. I wonder how hungry the coyotes are this time of year, just past winter. My breath quickens, and a loss of self-control begins to overtake me. At the moment when it seems I will be overrun by fear, my feet hit the planks of a narrow wooden bridge that crosses the creek bordering my aunt and uncle's property. The mailbox and turn off to their house aren't far now, and I can make out the yellow beacon of light from their porch.

I let myself in and embrace the warmth and security of a place I loved visiting as a teen. I sense Aunt Cora's comforting presence when I smell the aroma of her freshly baked bread and see the colorful jars of homemade jam on her kitchen counter. The well-oiled wooden floorboards and walnut furniture reflect Uncle Pete's loving touches and add to the sense of a stable, solid home. I let the atmosphere of this much-needed harbor of refuge sink in. I'm exhausted from the day's events, but it's not a physical fatigue. My climb to the attic room where I slept peacefully as a teen is burdened by fears of inheriting a self-destructive legacy from my father, and I don't sleep much.

The next day, I find Aunt Cora in the kitchen when I give up on sleep and go down the stairs. "Morning, Valerie. How 'bout some breakfast?"

"Thanks, Aunt Cora, but I'm not hungry." I get some coffee and take a seat at the table. She leans over and wraps her arms around me. "Your mom isn't ready to go back," she tells me. "It's hard for her to think about being all by herself in your father's house."

"Oh, I thought she wanted to drive back with me."

"Pete and I will drive her home when she's ready."

"Aunt Cora, it seems to me that, for the first time in a long time, Mom was happy here with you, Uncle Pete, and her job. Why is she going home?"

"She needs to take care of probate issues with the county."

"Will she be okay by herself when she gets home?"

"Valerie, your mom talked to me about asking you to return home now that Paul won't be there."

My eyes widen, my jaw drops open, and the coffee's acidic contents churn my stomach.

Aunt Cora sees my distress. "Valerie dear, I reminded your mother that you're an adult and may want to keep your apartment. Pete and I will do what we can to help her during this tough time. Your mom was there for me when I was young, and I owe her for how she protected me from your grandfather. We'll be here for you, too."

I'm puzzled by the information. "What happened with Granddad?"

Aunt Cora looks away and gathers her thoughts. "I believe he molested your mom. I don't know that for sure because your mom holds so much inside rather than talk. She never talked about what our dad did to her, but she made sure I didn't get hurt."

"Is that why you stand up for her?"

"Valerie, your mom had a very tough time before your granddad died. She needs to live her life with black-and-white morals, and she relies on straight-forward cultural dictates, the sayings that you call fortune-cookie sayings. It was how she managed to get through whatever our dad did to her."

Mom's rigidness and inability or refusal to discuss an issue begin to make some sort of sense. Her ability to do the mechanical aspects of parenting like feed and clothe without any deeper bonding also makes more sense to me as I listen to Aunt Cora. My face relaxes, and I decide to eat something so I toast some bread and select a jar of strawberry jam.

As I eat, Aunt Cora tells me the weather forecast is clear and roads should be dry as I return home. After a bit of hesitation, she continues, "Pete said you two talked about Paul's time in Vietnam." She gets up, pulls a sheathed knife from a drawer, and places it on the table in front of me.

"What's that?"

"It's your dad's bayonet from the M16 rifle he used in Vietnam."

It's a stark, physical reminder of Dad at war. Aunt Cora says, "Your dad gave this to Pete years ago for safekeeping because he feared he would use it on someone if he kept it handy."

A chilly wave sweeps through me as I remember how often Dad threatened me with a kitchen knife when he got drunk.

"Oh, dear. Maybe this isn't the best time to give this to you. Still, after your talk with Pete last night, he thought you should have it."

I'm not sure I want it, but its connection to Dad and what he suffered in war overrides my caution. I snap the army-green scabbard open, grip the black, textured hilt, and remove the bayonet. The 7-inch blade, designed for a stabbing thrust, reminds me of its deadly design.

"Aunt Cora, this bayonet holds scary memories. I'm not sure I want it."

Aunt Cora asks, "What did you use to get a loaf of bread ready for the toaster?"

I'm confused by the question. Then, she asks, "What did you use to spread the jam?"

I look at the serrated knife I used to cut bread and at the butter knife I used to spread jam and begin to understand what my aunt suggests.

"Sweetie, many things can be either helpful or harmful depending on how they are used. Knives, for instance, can be used to slice bread and spread strawberry jam while also having the capacity to rip savagely into someone's body or soul. Paul's bayonet can represent many things, and it's up to you what meaning to give it."

I decide to take Dad's bayonet and wonder what meaning I'll eventually assign to it. After Aunt Cora's explanation of Mom's conduct, I'll also think about what meaning to give Mom's high school ring, the one she gave me at Christmas.

I need to leave, get home, and go back to work. I'm also anxious to return and be with Kurt, so I take the bayonet and decide that, when I unpack, I'll put it with Mom's class ring.

Before leaving, I peek into Mom's room. Her back is toward the door, and I'm not sure she's awake. "Mom, I need to leave." There's no movement. She hasn't spoken to me since she accused me of contributing to Dad's death. Mom's silence gives me a sense of being erased or even disappearing from her and from life itself.

Ch. 14 – The Addict's Web

FEAR, LIKE AN UNSHEATHED NERVE, fires shots of pain through my soul during the drive home. I'm fueled with enough raw emotion to ignite road rage should some other driver do me wrong. Knowledge about Dad's heroin use rides front and center in my mind. My new understanding of Dad's impact on my life makes my internal demons act like prisoners shaking bars of a cage as they seek some form of parole, and I know where to get a reprieve for them.

When I see the sign that indicates my off-ramp is only two miles away, I decide against exiting the freeway near my apartment and drive a few exits farther to the one that will take me to Kurt's place. I'm sure, under the circumstances, Alice won't mind caring for Bean a couple more days so I can spend the weekend with Kurt.

I drive to Kurt's gated complex where the guard gets the okay to let me in and gives me a pass to hang from the rearview mirror. In the visitors' parking area, I turn off the engine and find that my hands shake as I affix the pass and open the door. I'm unnerved by what I am thinking.

When I step out of my car, an icy wind howls off Lake Erie and sends leaves into a whirlwind near my feet. I pull my parka close and walk toward the welcoming warmth of Kurt's building. Although I'm in familiar surroundings, my fears about Dad's legacy signal my arrival in foreign terrain.

I enter the vestibule, dial Kurt's suite, and get buzzed into the lobby. I nod to the desk clerk as I cross the marble floor to the elevators. On Kurt's floor, I'm relieved to see him waiting for me in the hallway and frightened by what I'm about to ask him. I ignore Kurt's inquiry about my drive home and say, "Kurt, I need you," as my inner demons scream, *I need your drugs!*

Kurt puts his arm around my waist as we walk into his unit. "How are you?"

It's a great question, but I don't want to answer.

"What's going on, Valerie? Are you okay?"

I'm not ready to talk about what's bothering me so I say, "Dad's memorial service was harder to get through than I thought it would be."

"I'm sorry I couldn't be there. What can I do?"

"How 'bout a hug?"

As we hug, I look over Kurt's shoulder at the piano I'm learning to play and at the cameras we use on outdoor adventures. Is it too late to embrace music, art, and love or does my family background make that impossible?

A whimper escapes my throat, and Kurt shushes me as he might a child. He moves his hands across my shoulders and back, but my inner turmoil wants a different type of relief. I close my eyes to avoid looking at the piano and cameras. *Who am I kidding when I dare to hope for a better life?*

My lips, near Kurt's ear, whisper, "Alice told me you shoot drugs. I could use a fix, and I don't want to snort it."

Kurt's hands stop their soothing movement on my back although his arms remain around me. I'm afraid he doesn't like what I said. He lets out a brief sigh, kisses my ear, and holds me close. When I'm about to retract my request, he releases me, goes to the hall closet, gets his leather jacket, reaches into the gun pocket, and gets the zippered pouch that I saw when he gave me some powder to snort several weeks ago.

He looks at me. "Valerie, I thought you would leave me if you knew about this. I'm glad you know."

I watch Kurt remove a bent spoon from the pouch and place it on the kitchen counter. He opens a small baggie, sprinkles some powder into the bowl of the spoon, and takes the cap off a small syringe. He goes to the sink, pulls some water up the needle, and squirts it into the shallow bowl where it mixes with the powder. He flicks open a lighter and heats the underside of the spoon to dissolve the powder with water before adding a bit of cotton. He uses the cotton to filter the mixture as he draws it up the fit, which is what Kurt calls the syringe.

Watching all this routine movement on Kurt's part, a dark routine that's alien to anything I've seen before, fascinates me at the same time that it warns me to back off and get the hell away. My brain tells me this is all wrong, but my inner turmoil focuses on what Kurt calls a fix. I'm scared but take comfort in knowing that Kurt shoots up frequently. If he uses narcotics intravenously, it can't be so bad, can it? Plus, when I snorted the stuff recently, I felt great. If it felt so right when inhaled, how could it be wrong to shoot it up?

When Kurt finishes preparing the drug, he looks at me. I see a gentle resignation on his face and detect compassion without reproach for what I am thinking about doing. His sympathy encourages me to smile and gives me a measure of courage.

Kurt points the needle end of the syringe up with one hand, uses his other hand to flick it with the back of a finger several times, and pushes the air out until a droplet forms at the tip. He lays the syringe down, tightens a flexible band around my arm, and raises a vein.

Kurt glances at my face before turning back to his task. He inserts the surgical needle into my arm and pulls the plunger back. Blood, my blood, moves up the syringe to mix with heroin. The sight of that bold red tint startles me, and I gasp. I hadn't anticipated seeing a streak of red enter the needle.

"Your blood means I found the vein."

Kurt looks up from my arm and asks, "Valerie, are you sure you want to do this? There's no turning back once I push this in."

My heart races, but I don't know if that's due to excited anticipation for what I'm thinking about doing or to fear that using heroin means I'm giving up on myself. I lower my eyes, purse my lips as my forehead tightens, and nod my head.

Kurt hesitates. My eyes are squeezed shut. I know that if I wait much longer, I'll chicken out. With eyes still closed tightly, I say, "Do it!"

I don't feel anything, open my eyes, and see the needle in my arm still filled with blood-tinted heroin. I look at Kurt who is studying me, so I take a deep breath and let it out slowly. I think about how my college failure torments me and about how my life options have narrowed to this surgically fine point of steel in my vein. I conclude that I need relief. A calming resolve settles in my mind, my face relaxes, and I tell Kurt in my normal voice, “Let’s do it.”

After I make that brief statement, I watch the liquid relief go from the syringe into my vein. Almost immediately, heroin weds itself to every cell of my being. The narcotic, both groom and honeymoon, carries me over a threshold far away from my troubles. The impact, the “rush,” evaporates all my problems in seconds.

My veins provide the means to cross over from a hellish birthright to nirvana. Mainlining heroin, the logical outcome toward which my family legacy has propelled me, is no accident of fate but fate’s official seal of approval for my matriculating properly along the path laid out for me at birth. Without pomp and circumstance, I march to my new position a yard or two over the line separating the mundane from the taboo.

My pupils constrict, my eyelids go half-mast, and I retreat into heroin’s cozy, downy sensation of absolute relief.

Part II

THE MASS of men lead lives of quiet desperation…

Henry David Thoreau, *Walden*, 1854

Ch. 15 - A Smooth Landing

HEROIN, NOW A WEEKEND HABIT, provides an effortless escape from facing myself and my family's legacy. No Berlin Wall needs to be scaled; no prison wire needs to be cut. I don't need to study piano notes, chords, or scales. I don't need to analyze camera shutter speeds or aperture settings. I don't have to hike in winter to watch the sun's rays sparkle through icicles onto prehistoric stone. I don't need to walk a humid jungle in a Glasshouse filled with enormous plants and exotic creatures. Most of all, I don't have to face my traumatic past or my failure to finish college. With heroin, all I need to do is let Kurt prepare the drug then shoot me up, an easy escape.

The drug fires up my brain's pleasure center with explosions of well-being that jet out to every cell in my body. Sure, there's some nausea and vomiting, but once my stomach is empty, I drop into the drug's embrace and float away. Everything feels fine until the drug wears off, and I crash into an irritable state in which I keep scratching at my skin. That discomfort passes quickly with the help of alcohol and marijuana.

It's always hard to ignore the desire to get high again, but I do. I resolve to shoot up only on weekends because I want to hold onto my Monday-through-Friday, 9-to-5 job. I'm confident that I can manage my heroin use.

Weekend trips into nirvana help me smile and interact more at work. Anointed with the fervor of a newly converted heroin user, an exalted status, I treat my uninitiated coworkers with compassion and love. I hang around the coffee machine, gossip, and take part in the March Madness basketball pool, activities that add to my sense of well-being and lessen my sense of being trapped in an office job.

My only problem is dealing with Mom. Ever since her return from West Virginia, she calls me every day to invite me to dinner. She cannot understand why I prefer going to my own place after work. During the week, I often hear my phone ringing as I walk down the apartment hallway to unlock my door and know from experience that it's Mom. I ignore her annoying calls but visit her after work once a week for dinner. She's very needy and has forgotten her accusation that I killed her husband.

Easter, the first holiday after Dad's death, becomes a problem for my mom and me. Kurt had planned a trip for us to visit his Dad in San Diego for the holiday weekend followed by a stay in Zion National Park. A week before Easter, I call Mom to remind her about my trip.

"Hi, Mom. How're you doing?"

"Humph, . . . since you never call, do you really care?"

I sigh because I called her only two days ago.

"I want to remind you that Kurt's taking me to San Diego for Easter weekend and then to Zion National Park for a vacation."

"So, I'll be alone on Easter."

Uh, oh.

"Well, you have a good time, Valerie. That's all that matters."

I want her off the phone and off my back. If I do not end this conversation fast, I'll need more than a drink to rekindle my excitement about flying for the first time, seeing a major West Coast city, and visiting one of the national parks with Kurt.

"I *will* have a good time. Goodbye, Mom."

She doesn't say anything, and I place the phone on its cradle. It rings almost instantly after the disconnect, but I don't answer. I wait for the intrusive sound to stop and then call Aunt Cora for advice. "Mom is driving me crazy," I blurt out.

Aunt Cora chuckles good-naturedly at my desperate outburst. "What's going on, sweetie?"

"I've made plans with Kurt for Easter and the week after, and Mom isn't happy about being alone for the holiday."

"Valerie, she doesn't need to be alone on Easter; Pete and I invited her to come here."

"Why is she staying home then?"

"I don't know."

My difficulty dealing with Dad's death prompts me to ask, "Is it possible that Mom is mourning Dad by staying in the house she inherited from him and wanting me to fill the void he left?"

"Sure, that could be part of what's going on with her."

"Aunt Cora, I feel bad for Mom and want to help, but I told her weeks ago about my and Kurt's trip to California and Utah." I pause a moment to reflect on how different my aunt and mother are. "Why are you and she so different? I wish you were my mom."

My aunt walks a tough line between her love for Mom, her sister, and me, her niece. I hear her take a deep breath before speaking. "Valerie, your Mom and I had such different experiences growing up. Whenever I ask her what happened between her and our dad, she goes silent behind the platitude, 'Don't speak ill of the dead'."

I'm still upset, don't want to hear my aunt defend Mom, and know I'm being childish when I say, "Yeah, she's great at spewing out trite, fortune-cookie clichés."

"Valerie, I wish things had been different for your mom. Whatever happened must have been terrible for her to have to hold so much inside."

My aunt's insights help put things into perspective. "You're right, Aunt Cora. I'll try to be more understanding."

"You and your mom will work things out, but you're young and have a wonderful opportunity to travel. Go, and I'll do what I can for your mom. She was always there for me when I was small, and I will be there for her. Pete and I will be here for you, too."

After hanging up the phone, I try to reignite some enthusiasm for my upcoming trip by opening a trail map of Zion, but I'm angry over how difficult my life is and cannot focus. It's tempting to get high, but I can't follow through because I don't have powder or syringe. Anyway, it's a work night, and I don't want to use drugs during the week. I give up trying to concentrate on my trip, open a bottle of spiced rum, and pour a hefty-sized portion into a tumbler.

Ch. 16 - San Diego Breezes

MEETING KURT'S FATHER rivaled the tension and excitement of flying for the first time. Upon arrival in San Diego, we are waiting for our bags to come down the shoot when Kurt tells me, "Dad should be here, but I don't see him."

Kurt still doesn't see his dad after we collect our luggage from the revolving dispenser.

"Maybe Dad's outside waiting for us in his car. Stay here while I take a look."

After Kurt walks away, a short man with salt-and-pepper hair removes what looks like a chauffeur's cap and puts his hand on one of our bags. "Miss, I assist. I take bag. My taxi just out door."

It's been only seven months since 9/11, and after dealing with all the new airport security, I'm wary of this offer from a man with a foreign accent, but he begins walking away with one of our bags. I'm not sure what to do and am relieved to see Kurt walking in our direction. He grabs the man from behind until the man lets go of our baggage. After Kurt releases him, the man spins around ready to strike.

"Kurt, look out!"

Kurt's arms fly up in self-defense, and I fear a brawl will begin. Instead of a fight, the two men embrace and begin patting each other on the back and laughing.

"This is my dad, but you gotta watch out, Valerie, because he's a big jokester."

Kurt's dad says, "Glad to meet the wee lassie who took me bairn's heart."

I'm confused. "Bairn?"

"He means child, a Scottish word. And, he tisn't no Scot, me da ain't." Now, Kurt is using an accent and speaking foreign-sounding words.

Kurt's dad gives me a warm, welcoming hug and says, "It *is* good to meet you, Valerie."

"It's nice to meet you, too, Mr. Wolfe."

Kurt's dad chuckles as he says, "Call me Skipper."

"Skipper, how did you know it was me when you grabbed my bag?"

He's laughing. "I watched you and Kurt from behind a pillar. Good thing security didn't pick me up for suspicious behavior."

Kurt bats Skipper's chest playfully. "If they had picked you up, it would've served you right for letting us wait so long!"

It's a short drive to Skipper's two-bedroom apartment on Crown Point Drive. The kitchen, dining, and living areas form one large room under a wood-beamed ceiling. One wall, made up of windows and a large patio door, provides a view of Mission Bay. In the distance, I can see Fiesta Island and downtown San Diego. The apartment reminds me of Kurt's condo, and I feel comfortable and at ease.

Kurt and I put our things away in the guest bedroom and go out to help Skipper set a table on the deck. As I lay napkins and flatware down on the patio table, I feel a warm breeze coming from the coastal wetland that stretches out and around the bay across the street. Skipper opens a bottle of chilled wine, hands it to Kurt who pours it into crystal wine glasses, and goes to the refrigerator. He returns with some platters of food.

When we sit down, Skipper asks about my cat, and I tell him about Alice who is taking care of Bean while I'm away. He listens attentively and asks good questions as I talk about my job. I glow under his approving gaze and open up to him as if we've known each other for a long time.

Kurt and his father need to talk about some business regarding the condominium, so after we eat, I stack the dishes in the dishwasher and leave them alone. It's been a long day, and I lie down in the guest bedroom, close my eyes, and fall asleep. I don't even stir when Kurt gets into bed sometime after midnight.

When I wake the next morning, Kurt is still asleep. I hear Skipper humming a Broadway tune in the shower, smell coffee, and decide to get up. I've learned not to startle Kurt while he's sleeping because that could trigger a flashback, so I ease myself out of bed.

I pour a cup of coffee and settle on the couch with a historical novel about two women—one, a contemporary woman, and the other from the 17th century.

Skipper walks by and heads for the coffee pot. "Morning, Valerie. What'cha reading?"

"*The Weight of Ink.*"

"Oh, I hear that the book's about people with too many tattoos."

My mouth drops before I catch myself and see him ready to laugh with me not at me. "Good one," I tell him in response to his good-natured teasing.

Skipper plates some fruit and pastries, refreshes our coffee mugs, and invites me to join him on the deck. The morning breeze carries hints of the Pacific Ocean, and we watch a lone kingfisher hover over the wetland. "It's a little late in the season for kingfishers, but it's still a beautiful sight," Skipper says as he hands me a pair of binoculars.

I find the kingfisher. "It's gorgeous."

Then, Skipper points out the snowy egrets, flashes of white in the marsh grass.

"Kurt tells me you're talented and smart."

I'm not sure how to respond.

"I bet you loved college."

Skipper's comment triggers thoughts that sadden me. "I did love school, but dropped out." I lower the binoculars, look down to my lap, and feel an urge to do drugs.

Skipper retrieves the binoculars and studies the wetland. "I remember being so homesick my first year away from home that I kept thinking about leaving college. Were you homesick when you left?"

Skipper's empathy and kindness bring my thoughts back to the lovely morning we're sharing. "I wasn't homesick."

Skipper sets down the binoculars, grabs a croissant, plates it, and hands it to me along with a napkin. His thoughtfulness suggests he might help rather than hurt me.

"I left because I was scared."

The confession doesn't provide relief; it stirs up uncomfortable emotions. I put the pastry down and stare into my coffee mug.

Skipper puts his arm around my shoulder and begins a gentle sway on the glider we're sharing. His calm voice asks, "What troubles you, Valerie?"

I look at him and am encouraged when I see something comforting and kind in his face so I tell him, "I dropped out rather than go to classes requiring presentations. Talking in class terrified me."

I told Kurt's dad the thing that sits sour in my psyche and eats at my soul. I feel ashamed and alone.

"When I got to law school, I felt the same about the oral arguments we had to do. I was scared and wanted to run away."

"But you became a lawyer, so you didn't run."

"I almost ran, but one of my professors understood how hard it is to speak in public. She told me that many, maybe most, people experience anything from brief anxiety to full-blown panic when confronted with public speaking. The fear is so common that an international club was founded, in part, to help people overcome speech anxiety."

"Did you join the club?"

"I did, and it helped me get over my speech apprehension. I bet there's a club near you." He chuckles good-naturedly as he says, "Geez, I sound like a commercial."

I laugh, too, because his last statement did sound preachy.

"Anyway, last night after you went to bed, Kurt and I talked about going for a sail today. I'm called Skipper for a reason, you know. How does getting out on Mission Bay sound?"

I'm relieved by the change in topic and say, "Sounds great."

I like being with Skipper and begin humming as the glider moves back and forth.

We hear Kurt in the shower.

Skipper says, "Good, he's up. Can you help me pack some gear and provisions for the day?"

"I'd love to."

While we pack a few items, Skipper's neighbor Barbara arrives. She has a cast on her arm which prevents me from shaking her hand when we're introduced.

Skipper explains, "Barbara tried doing the can-can in a dance class at the senior center and fell on her can-can. That's how she broke her wrist."

Barbara takes a friendly swat at Skipper, but it's clear from her laughter that she loves his teasing.

Kurt joins us and meets Barbara. "Dad's told me a lot about you. I'm glad we're finally meeting."

After finding a pushcart at the marina, we take our gear from the car and wheel it to Skipper's slip.

"This little Pacific Seacraft is the love of my life," says Skipper as he helps Barbara board his 24-foot boat. The sailboat's classic lines and long stretches of teak make it stand out from the other boats at the marina.

I get on the boat, and Kurt hands me our provisions. After everything is on board and stowed, Kurt begins removing the dock lines that tether the boat to land.

As Skipper warms up the diesel engine, Barbara says, "I usually do some of the prep work, but can't with this stupid cast."

"Tell me what to do, and I'll do it," I say. Under Barbara's guidance, I remove the sail cover, fold it, and put it down in the salon. Skipper opens what he calls a halyard, hands it to me, and tells me where to attach it to the mainsail. As he takes the slack out of the line to the sail, he says, "Good job, Valerie."

We're ready to go, and Kurt steps aboard to remove the last line connecting us to the marina. Skipper puts the boat into reverse and moves from the dock as Kurt and I push the boat away from the pilings. Once clear of the dock, Skipper uses the forward gear to move us out of the marina and into open water.

I sit near the helm and settle back to enjoy the scenery. Skipper noses into the wind, and Kurt raises the mainsail. I watch Skipper and Kurt angle the boat to catch the wind. The sail curves into the shape of a ballerina's slipper, and the boat heels a few degrees away from center.

Then, Skipper cuts the noisy engine, and everything changes because the boat begins a silent, magical dance that makes my spirit soar. I've never been so easily transported from the everyday to what feels sacred by anything other than drugs before this experience with sailing. Something inside me changes, and although I can't identify what changed, I'm energized, exhilarated, and captivated.

Skipper lets me steer once we are out on open water. When I take the tiller, I'm delighted to feel the boat come alive in my hand. I can feel the breeze and ocean swells telegraphed from boat to my fingers. I put enough tension on the rudder to feel like I'm holding the world's winds, currents, and unfathomable mysteries at my fingertips.

Skipper helps me point into the wind so the foresail can be unfurled. Then, he shows me how to set a course on the autohelm. Once we establish a point of sail, Kurt takes my hand and we move to the front or bow of the boat. We dangle our legs over the side near the bowsprit, a narrow platform that points seaward. Kurt says, "This is my favorite spot under sail."

I immediately know why. The soothing sound of water slithers along the hull a few yards below our bare feet. As the bow encounters small swells, we ride a gentle rocking motion that's a delight. The rhythm of the boat on the waves connects us to the pulse, if not the heartbeat, of the planet.

After a half-hour or so, Barbara comes forward. "Skipper wants to set a new course and needs your help at the helm, Kurt."

When Kurt leaves, Barbara and I move back a few feet and put our backs against the cabin. "What a lovely day," she says.

For a while, we enjoy the breeze before she tells me. "Skipper worries about Kurt although he tries not to show it."

I like Skipper and want to help him if I can. "What worries him?"

"Kurt was prescribed opioids after returning from the Gulf War."

"Yeah, I know. A lot of vets were."

"Yes, true." Barbara sighs and thinks a moment before continuing. "Skipper is afraid Kurt may be getting prescriptions from more than one doctor and taking too many pills."

"Barbara, I like Kurt and Skipper a lot, but I'm not sure what you're asking of me."

"Valerie, dear, I'm not sure either." She pats my hand, gets up, and goes aft.

I worry about Kurt's drug use, too, especially now that I'm doing drugs along with him, but sailing in warm ocean breezes under blue skies won't allow me to think about troubles. I'm grinning as I return to the cockpit, and Skipper gives me command of the boat. I love capturing the wind, gliding among the waves, and feeling the spray on my face. I'm hooked.

Ch. 17 - Angel's Landing at Night

A FEW DAYS LATER, Kurt and I are hiking the predawn darkness at Zion National Park. The park closes overnight to everyone except lodge guests and those with backcountry passes. We see no one else out and about this early. The trail we are on takes us to a pedestrian bridge where we cross the Virgin River. On the other side of the river, we take the Kayenta Trail on the left. The quiet, windless morning forms a companionable presence, and we watch rays of light bounce off the snow-capped mountains as the sun begins to rise.

"I wish Dad was here," Kurt says. "He would love this."

I take Kurt's hand and tell him, "I like your dad."

"Yeah, he's a great guy." Then, Kurt mumbles, "He deserves a better son than me."

I look at Kurt and don't ask about what he said because his face looks sad and closed off.

After about a mile, the path curves away from the river to travel upward. It's an easy trek that doesn't aggressively climb toward mountain peaks. A mist moves along the top of the massive sandstone walls, and the red-tinted soil on the trail mirrors the color of gigantic summits on our right. The lovely view lifts Kurt's mood, and he squeezes my hand.

We turn a bend and make an abrupt stop. In the distance, water tumbles from fissures in the sandstone into pools far below. The silence, the beauty, the massive rock, and the waterfall force gasps of wonder from my lips. My eyes moisten and a sob jets out from my throat as I internalize the sacred, ancient essence of this place.

Kurt and I stand side-by-side in silent reverence, an arm around each other.

After a few moments, I whisper, "This feels better than. . ." and Kurt finishes my thought with the word, "drugs." He pulls me closer, and I lay my head against his shoulder.

We take a trail that leads to three waterfalls and watch the runoff leap down from massive, rocky heights. Trees, dwarfed into supplicants at the mountain's base, stand over us, but the splendor around us does not make us feel small or insignificant. Instead, I experience being a part of all the wonder that surrounds us.

The spiritual connection to this place begins to diminish when we hear bus engines growling through the valley. The park entrance gates must have opened. The trail we are on loops back to the lodge, and we soon pass groups of people, many speaking foreign languages, as we head back to our room.

In the lodge, we spend the day resting and getting ready for an evening hike. After dinner, we strap on backpacks and hike a different trail than the one we walked in the morning. For the first half-mile or so, we travel against a flow of people returning to the main road where they will catch the last buses out of the park. By the time we get to Walter's Wiggles, a series of steep switchbacks, we are alone on the trail and begin the 1,000-foot climb to Scout Lookout.

When we reach the lookout, a flat area where hikers can continue to Angel's Landing, we switch on our headlamps. We decide against going further because the climb involves using rock-embedded chains to scramble up and across a high, razorback ridge. It's too risky to tackle that last half-mile in the dark to get to Angel's Landing, almost 1500 feet above the canyon floor.

We settle down under a thermal blanket, put our backs against a sandstone abutment, and pull on knit caps and insulated gloves. Nights are chilly at this altitude, but the cold sharpens our view of the Milky Way.

Kurt opens a thermos of coffee. "I saw you and Barbara talking at the bow of the boat during our sail. What did you two talk about?"

I take a bite of an energy bar. "She said Skipper worries about you and your prescriptions."

"Yeah, I know. He tried to help me stop using those drugs before he moved to San Diego. I don't think he suspects I'm also using a needle now. If he knew about that, I'm afraid it would kill him."

Kurt sips his coffee before adding, "I was in Desert Storm."

The change in topic puzzles me. I look at Kurt, but he doesn't look back. His gaze is an odd combination of being distant yet close and internal.

"I often have nightmares about being lost in the Iraqi desert. In those dreams, I see armored tanks and think I'm being rescued only to discover that the tanks try to bury me alive. When I was in Iraq, I saw arms and legs sticking out where our tanks had pushed sand over enemy trenches. Some Iraqi soldiers had been buried alive."

In hoarse tones, Kurt says, "On the Highway of Death from Kuwait, I saw bodies charred and solidified into agonized shapes, mummified in their attempts to flee. They were enemies, sure, but they were human beings, too. In other nightmares, I wake up terrified that I'm about to be scorched to death during battle."

Kurt's voice breaks. "Later, . . . a report comes out . . . almost 25 percent of our casualties . . . were killed by us, . . . by friendly fire."

His voice strengthens. "I hate the term. What's so friendly about being killed by your own troops or killing them like they were enemies? I may have accidentally killed one of my buddies, and it's something too awful to think about."

Kurt takes another sip of coffee. "It was so confusing. We were fighting with little sleep, often at night, and smoke from burning oil wells and bombed military equipment was everywhere. I can't shake images of what I saw and what I may have done."

Kurt shifts position and puts his coffee mug on a flat strip of rock.

"I have lots of trouble sleeping; my muscles and joints hurt, too. A doctor prescribed an opioid. After a year or so, I got another doctor to prescribe the pills so I could double my dose. At first, doctors said the pills weren't addictive."

Kurt struggles to keep his voice even. "At one point, I learned I could crush the pills into a powder and inject them for faster relief. Last year, when it got harder to get both prescriptions, I started using heroin, too."

Kurt blurts out, "I don't know how to stop using, and I don't know how to stop the nightmares about the war."

"Kurt, I wasn't in the military, but I've been hurt by war, too. Don't wars come home when their soldiers come home and affect those who weren't there?"

Kurt lowers his head onto my shoulder. "I don't want to hurt you, Valerie, and I'm afraid I'm hurting my dad by using."

We go quiet, and a movement in the brush diverts our attention, but it's only a chipmunk.

"Kurt, this mountain range has been forced into existence by some massive, prehistoric upheaval yet it is now filled with a positive spirit. Do you think it's possible that human pain can also get transformed into something positive?"

Kurt looks thoughtful. "You know, I like thinking about that. It gives me hope that I can change, too."

I take a sip of coffee and look to the sky.

"Kurt, I have never seen so many stars before."

Kurt looks up, and a shooting star brings him back from his thoughts about foreign deserts.

Our headlamps, switched to red to protect our night vision, catch sight of a mule deer munching in the brush. We keep some bear spray on hand in case of unwanted critters but nothing more threatening than chipmunks come near us.

Kurt asks, "What did you and my dad talk about when you two were on the patio glider?"

Wow, now it's my turn to spit out a dark secret.

"I feel trapped in a boring job."

"Trapped? Why not get a different job?"

"Kurt, I don't want a different job. I want to go back to school."

"What's stopping you, Valerie? Money?"

My face tightens because I'd rather not talk about what's bothering me. I manage to say, "It ain't money. I'm scared."

Kurt waits. He knows the struggle of wrestling with personal demons.

"I don't think I deserve better, and I'm terrified of talking in class. If I speak up and call attention to myself, then I might be attacked. I know it's irrational, but it's scary."

I know exactly when I began having trouble in school and decide to tell Kurt about it. "One winter day, I was working on a term paper for freshman English when Dad demanded that I help him fix his car. My hair was wet from the shower, but I couldn't ask him to wait until I dried it. I always had to shut up and put up, so I pulled on a knit hat and went out into the cold."

Even though it's chilly where we are near Angel's Landing, I begin sweating and trembling. Kurt hugs me closer.

"Dad was mad about his car and kept yelling at me like it was my fault he couldn't get it started. When he gave up on fixing the car and started throwing his tools at me, I gave up, too, and felt scared all the time. Speaking in class and being the center of attention were out of the question, so I dropped classes that required active participation. After that semester, I gave up on school altogether."

"What can I do to help, Valerie?"

I sigh. "I don't know. Your dad told me about a speech club. He said it might help me overcome my fears so that I can go back to school."

I slump against Kurt's shoulder feeling exhausted by my confession.

Kurt points to the east where the sky is getting lighter. We hadn't planned on staying all night and hadn't noticed how the stars were disappearing as we talked.

"The thing I want most is to go back to school."

"And, I want to quit using drugs so much when we get home."

The lilt had returned to Kurt's voice, and he's smiling again so I ask, "Do you think we can help each other do those things?"

Kurt thinks awhile. "We can try. Dad would want me to get counseling, maybe you could try it, too."

"Maybe."

"I need to do something, Valerie. Dad told me he doesn't plan to return to Cleveland, and he found a buyer for the condo. I need to be out in a couple of months, mid-June at the latest."

"Wow, that sucks. You don't have much time to find a place and move."

"Yeah, I know."

We turn off our headlamps, pack our things, and begin the descent from our spot near Angel's Landing. At the base of Zion's mountains, the cathedral-like canyon reinforces my hope that Kurt and I can find a way out of the things that drive our drug use. There are demons to face when we get back from our vacation.

Ch. 18 - The Tipping Point

THE FORCES DRIVING OUR SELF-DESTRUCTIVE tendencies destroy our good intentions when we return from Zion National Park to our everyday lives. We thought we could change, but we underestimated the strength of our dark, internal motivations to harm ourselves.

My good intentions collapse several days after being home when Mom phones and stirs up old fears and insecurities.

"Oh, you're finally home."

"Hi, Mom."

"I thought you fell off a cliff or something since you haven't called."

"I'm fine, Mom. How're you?"

"Well, since I never hear from you anymore, I didn't think you cared." I had called her between connections on our flight home three days ago.

"I thought that having your father's car would make it easier for you to visit me. I guess you have better places to drive to than to your mother's house."

I visited her before leaving when I treated her to a meal at her favorite restaurant and gave her an Easter lily. Unpacking, doing laundry, and restocking the refrigerator ate up my time since returning home.

My jaw tightens as I listen to Mom whine. She's alone and punishes herself by staying in that awful house when she could be living with her sister instead.

"I guess Kurt is better company than your own mother."

My voice surfaces like a bubble released from the bottom of a lake and gains force as it rises up my throat. I yell out, "Did you call to find out how I am, or did you call to complain?"

The outburst feels right, at least for a brief moment. Then, I hear sniffling, and Mom's voice breaks as she says, "how . . . can you . . . talk to me like that? All I want is for you to be happy."

I can't think of a reply that won't sound mean, so I retreat inside myself. I let her ramble on and on about her housework, what she ate for breakfast, and all sorts of trivial things. It's a running monologue with no room for me, but it's what she wants, and I allow her to verbally run over me.

As her voice fires away, I take the phone from my ear and hold it at arm's length for five minutes to find out if she notices I'm not listening. She doesn't notice. I might as well disappear. I sense that I'm becoming smaller and insignificant as she rambles on.

Finally, she includes me. "Will you be coming for dinner Wednesday?"

"Yeah, sure."

"Well, don't sound so excited, Valerie."

I want her off the phone. "See you then. Bye, Mom."

I set the phone down and sit hunched over peering at the floor. There's no way I can stand up enough for myself to get over my fears and return to school. My desire to change stands out for what it is – a threadbare, gossamer ghost. I call Kurt, "Can we do some smack this weekend?"

"Yeah. Sure thing, Valerie."

"So, no problem copping?"

I haven't used narcotics since before our trip and wasn't sure we still had a good connection.

"No. Your neighbors, Mitch and Janet, have stuff to deal."

It's Monday night, a long way until the weekend, but I'm in control of my heroin habit enough to wait. Some weeknight weed and hard liquor will get me through until Friday, so I light a joint and pour a tumbler of rum.

For several weeks, I teeter on a razor-sharp line separating my work week from weekend heroin use. Then, an early morning call from my mother in late April knocks me off balance.

"Valerie, I want you to live here and think about going back to school. You could quit working."

It's only Monday morning, and I'm not quite awake. I feel strung out from the weekend's drug use and am waiting for some coffee to get into my system. I need to get ready for work and can't deal with Mom right now.

"I won't take no for an answer," Mom bellows.

She will take no for an answer; I hang up on her. Mom never listened when I tried to tell her how badly Dad treated me or how scared I am to go back to school. She doesn't understand and doesn't want to.

The phone begins ringing, and I ignore it. The sound makes me pull my arms around myself and hunch over. Feeling trapped by my fears creates a sickening wave of bile. I run for the toilet where I go down on my haunches. When the heaving stops, I crawl to the bathroom wall, twist around, sit and pant like a cornered animal. I'm tempted to go across the hall, get a needle and some powder from Mitch and Janet, and fuck the day off. Instead, I call in sick and drive to Kurt's place.

"I'm taking the day off," I tell him as I barge into his condo. He just returned from his night shift, his pupils pinpoints. He looks high.

I know I *should* ask for comforting words instead of asking for drugs. I know I *should* be at work instead of being here wanting relief from a needle. I shove away all thoughts about what I *should* do and insist, "I need a fix."

Kurt doesn't ask why. He knows the balm of narcotics too well to fault me for my need. There's no heroin, but he crushes up some pills and injects me.

As I nod off next to him, I tell myself that missing one day of work to drugs is no big deal.

Ch. 19 - The Deep End

BOLTS OF LIGHTNING DAGGER INTO Lake Erie as thunder rumbles through Kurt's building. Tremors move across the floor, and the windows resonate with a low hum. April's icy winds have turned into a series of strong May storms.

Foul weather keeps me and Kurt indoors, and we plan on getting high all weekend. I'm as excited about doing the drugs as I am about seeing Kurt. If I'm honest, I may be here more for the narcotics than for Kurt.

I hunger as I watch Kurt prepare the needle, and I eagerly pump up a vein for my fix. It's a strong powder. When he hits me up, unconsciousness like a juggernaut is so fast that I don't even sense its approach. By the time Kurt removes the syringe, I've tumbled away from the world.

Darkness?

How deeply I sank into a dark tunnel is unknown.

How long?

Time passes by without me as a passenger.

Survival?

I am lucky, and at some point, I reconnect to the world when I force my eyes open. Everything is hazy so I keep blinking my eyelids. My jaw moves around as my mind struggles to awaken from its blank state. It's a mental battle to regain awareness of my surroundings and to physically feel like I've re-entered my body. I discover I'm prone on a couch and barely able to move. My foggy brain wonders whose couch I'm on.

When the room comes into focus, my mind seeks an explanation. I remember doing some drugs. *Weed? Did I smoke too much weed?* As my thoughts come up out of a fog, I remember it wasn't weed but heroin. Kurt's condominium comes into focus.

I move my arms and legs so that I can sit up. My mouth is cottony and my tongue sits useless in my mouth. Lack of saliva makes swallowing difficult, but I manage a hoarse whisper, "Kurt?"

There's no answer. *Am I alone? Abandoned?* Terrified, I force out one word, "KURT!"

"I'm right here." I turn my head in the direction of the voice and see Kurt by the counter that separates the kitchen from the living room. He gets a glass, fills it with water, and brings it to me.

"Here, this should help," he says as he hands me the glass. My hands aren't steady, and I grip the glass with both hands to drink without spilling the liquid.

"How are you feeling?"

I don't know how to answer that question because I'm not sure. I don't feel high, only woozy, but something nags at the back of my mind and forces out an unsavory conclusion.

"Kurt, I passed out." A mental red flag goes up, and I add, "I could have died. Why didn't you call 9-1-1?"

"You had a pulse; you were breathing."

Kurt's clinical answer does not help me feel better. He has some medical training from the Army, but I'm not convinced that his decision about not calling emergency was the correct one.

"How long did you check on me before shooting up?"

The long pause on Kurt's part is loud with his own cold regrets and my fear that his need for drugs meant I could have died. The stinging silence makes me realize how wrong, how dead wrong this is. Horror at what could have happened shoots through me.

"Valerie, you're right. I should have waited before shooting up and taking a chance on myself. After you . . ." Kurt can't finish the sentence.

Wow. He didn't wait long to make sure I was okay.

"Kurt, what if that fix sent you out, too? We could've both died."

A dark gap in our relationship forms as we grapple with what our drug habit is doing to us as a couple. When Kurt speaks, his voice is shallow. "I couldn't wait." He begins to cry.

"I wish . . ." Kurt wipes away some tears, takes a deep breath, and blurts out, "I wish I never started taking drugs. I can't stop. You're right. You could have died; we both could have died."

The truth makes me turn away from him even though I know another truth: I don't think I can stop using either.

Kurt says, "Drugs have ruined every relationship I've had. Now, this shit is hurting you, too."

He's right, and I know I should leave him before I really get hurt. But, leave him? Leaving him would mean leaving heroin, too. I can't face this possibility so I turn back to Kurt and say, "Look, I'm okay. You're fine, too. I'm sure my passing out was only a fluke, and it won't happen again."

I try to take comfort in my own words but wonder if I can keep from being drawn into a deadly web of addiction. I sense that I'm swirling dangerously close to a drain hole over which I'll have little control.

Ch. 20 - Cardiac Arrest

I IGNORE THE JARRING SOUND of my phone on the nightstand. It's early June, and I'm getting ready to leave for work. Anyway, it's probably Mom who often phones early.

Then, I hear Kurt's troubled voice on the answering machine.

"Dad . . . is . . . in hospital."

I snatch up the phone. "What happened?"

"I'm not sure." Kurt pauses, and I hear him inhale with a wavering sound. I know he's struggling to be able to tell me about Skipper. "Dad had trouble breathing and passed out. Luckily, Barbara was with him and got help right away. It's his heart. Looks like he suffered a cardiac arrest, and it's serious."

"Oh, no." I put my hand on my chest and sit on the bed. "How's he doing?"

"He's stable now, but they won't know about brain damage for a while."

"When will you know more?"

"Not sure. Maybe this afternoon."

"Kurt, are you okay?"

"I'm worried about him, Valerie."

"Kurt, I'm leaving for work but will come over as soon as I can. I'm sure I'll be able to leave early, probably before lunch. Hold on a few hours until I get there, okay?"

"Hurry, please."

Kurt doesn't sound good, and I am as worried about him as I am about his father. Before leaving for work, I put out enough food and water for Bean to get her through a day or two if that becomes necessary.

My boss has a mid-morning board meeting at another company and says he won't be back in the office until tomorrow. I get permission to leave early and arrive at Kurt's place around 11:00 a.m. Security has my name, and I pass into the condominium complex quickly.

When Kurt opens his door, we hold each other for several minutes. I rub his back and try to get a sense of how he's handling the news. When we step apart and I get a good look at him, I see that his face is puffy and he looks very tired. He also looks very stoned.

I ask if he's heard anything about his dad since this morning, and he has trouble updating me. "Barbara called 911 and did CPR until the ambulance arrived. A neighbor even grabbed a hallway defibrillator to use while waiting for the EMT's."

Then, Kurt blurts out the worst part, "It wasn't fast enough. Dad's brain suffered some damage from lack of oxygen."

"Oh, no." Tears form in my eyes as I realize the change this must mean for Skipper and for Kurt. I try to guide Kurt to the couch but he doesn't want to sit. He paces around the condo gathering things to pack.

"I have an early flight tomorrow so I can be with him."

"I'll drive you to the airport before I go to work. What else can I do?"

Kurt doesn't answer, and I feel helpless. I cook some pasta and toss a salad for something to do, but neither of us wants to eat.

Kurt calls to get an update from Barbara, a woman who doesn't sugarcoat the situation. She tells Kurt that Skipper's prognosis is good but he'll need nursing home care. Kurt will need to get a power of attorney so he can make medical, financial, and legal decisions for his father until Skipper can do this for himself. It's a lot for Kurt to take in, and I hear fear in his voice when he says, "I'm not sure I can make good decisions for Dad."

"You can do that, Kurt. Besides, Barbara will be there to help. I'll do what I can, too."

I can see how overwhelmed Kurt is and how difficult it is for him to figure out what to do. He takes a toiletry bag into the bathroom, returns to the living room, tosses the small bag into his suitcase, and sits down next to me where he nods out. I look at him and wonder if he did some heroin when he was in the bathroom. I give him a little shake, and he opens his eyes.

"What?"

His pupils are pinpoint tiny, but this isn't the time to call him out on his drug use or why he didn't offer to share.

"Come on. Why don't we go to bed?"

We move to the bedroom and Kurt curls up beside me. I put my arm around him and plant a kiss in his hair. He pulls away from me to lie on his side, head turned away.

Somehow, I drift asleep while wondering how to help and slip into a dream about searching for something or someone in a foggy forest. Then, I hear a voice calling, "Where am I?" The fog is thick, and I can't see who's calling out. I hear the voice again, louder. "*WHERE AM I?*" My eyes open, and I hear the same question in a whispered, pleading whimper, "Where am I?" It's Kurt's voice. He's not in bed. I sit up and turn on a light.

"Help me!"

The voice is coming from the bathroom. I leap out of bed, run the few steps to the master bath, and open the door. The windowless room goes tomb dark at night if the light is off and the door closed. I turn on a light and see Kurt on the floor next to the toilet lying in his own vomit.

There's some blood on Kurt's arm. He must've shot up and gotten sick. He's confused but recognizes me. I help him get up from the floor, walk into the bedroom, and put on clean pajamas. He gets back in bed, but I'm angry as I wipe up the puke he left in the bathroom. Kurt is falling apart at the time his father needs him.

I'm too worked up to sleep and spend the early morning hours checking now and then to be sure Kurt is breathing. He seems deep asleep or passed out. I have no way to know the difference and am too tired, too angry, to figure it out.

After sunrise, I wake Kurt so he can get ready for his flight to San Diego. He shakes his head when I ask if he wants breakfast, so we grab his carry-on bag and leave without eating or making coffee. As I drive Kurt to the airport, I debate whether to ask about what happened during the night. It's a relief when Kurt brings it up.

He sounds weary and defeated. "I don't like how you saw me last night in the bathroom."

I didn't like finding him in his vomit and not knowing where he was, but I don't say anything.

My lips compress in anger, and I sense that if we talk, we would hurt each other. I'm relieved to see the sign for the airport so I can exit the highway and leave Kurt off.

When Kurt gets out at the drop-off area and turns to look at me, I don't like what I see. His eyes are vacant and set back in dark circles. His cheeks are hollow, and he hunches over as he pulls his wheeled travel bag across the concrete and through the sliding doors. I can't linger. Airport security waves me off, so I drive away and head to the office.

My boss puts me to work as soon as I arrive at my desk. While typing some letters, I wonder how Kurt is doing. Around lunchtime, I get concerned because Kurt hadn't called between his connecting flights. In the middle of the afternoon, I get a call from the police.

"Are you Valerie Willis?"

"Yes."

"Airport police, Officer Rogers speaking. We found your contact information among Kurt Wolfe's things"

"Is he okay?"

"Mr. Wolfe was stumbling around the airport in an incoherent state. He acted drunk and didn't go through airport security. He spent the day in a police substation sobering up. We need to release him to a relative or friend. Otherwise, he gets sent to the county's mental services for evaluation."

"I'll come pick him up."

When I tell my boss that I have an emergency and need to leave, he isn't happy but lets me go. After taking care of Kurt during the night, cleaning up his vomit, and not sleeping, I'm tempted to forget about him and drive home, but I don't. Instead, I pull into the parking facility next to the police substation.

Inside, the officers tell me that Kurt was so terrified of flying that he drank a large amount of whiskey before trying to get to his flight. I'm not sure they believe that story from Kurt, but they were good-natured enough to indicate belief. I thank them for their help while Kurt gives them a silly, little-boy grin and shrugs as he follows me out the door.

When we're in my car, I demand, "Kurt, what happened?"

"I don't want to talk about it."

"We're not going anywhere until you tell me what happened."

I wait for his response, my hands gripping the steering wheel.

"I had a syringe and some powder hidden in my carry-on bag." He stops talking without explaining why he was with the police and why they let him leave.

"And?"

"I forgot about the new airport screening."

It hasn't yet been a year since 9/11, and airport security keeps evolving and tightening.

"I went into a restroom to get rid of the stuff and ended up mainlining it instead of tossing it out. I guess I took too much."

"You GUESS! What about your flight? What about your dad?" I'm furious.

"Stop it, Valerie. I feel bad enough about letting my dad down without you getting on me."

"What about letting me down? I care about you and your dad. Now, this is all screwed up, and so are you." I know I'm being hard on Kurt, harsher than I should be under the circumstances, but Kurt's erratic behavior pushes me into being the type of girlfriend I don't want to be.

I'm so angry that I drop Kurt at his place without staying. Kurt's life is out of control, which is making my life chaotic. Next time, if there is one, Kurt can clean up his own vomit.

I get take-out pizza on my way home and look forward to a quiet meal and some rest. After eating a couple of slices, I curl up by an open window with Bean purring in my lap. A warm breeze moves across my shoulders and carries the scent of lilacs from the bushes in front of the building. I relax and open a mystery novel but get interrupted when the phone rings. I expect to hear Kurt's voice when I pick up.

"Valerie. Hi. It's Barbara, Skipper's friend."

"Yes. Hi. How is Skipper?"

There's a slight pause before she answers. The situation is difficult for her, too.

"He can communicate a bit although it's not easy for him to form words."

I'm wondering why Barbara is calling me instead of Kurt, but I don't have to wait long to find out.

"What happened to Kurt? He never arrived."

"He missed his flight. Didn't he call you?"

"I haven't heard from him, and he's not answering his phone."

I take a deep breath and close my eyes.

Barbara asks, "What's going on?"

As I exhale, I tell her, "I don't know why he hasn't called you, but I'll try to find out."

I get Kurt's voicemail when I call. "Kurt, are you okay? Where are . . ."

"What do *you* want?" Kurt's harsh voice interrupts my questions.

"I . . . I . . ." it's hard to know what to say. "Chill. I'm on your side, Kurt."

"Yeah, right."

Kurt's voice is angry and slurred from too much alcohol or drugs or both.

"Ya wanna know what's going on, do you? Well, it's SCA. Yeah, *that's* what's going on."

This isn't making sense. "SCA?"

"Yeah, SCA or sudden cardiac arrest."

"Kurt, I don't understand."

"No, you don't. Well, Valerie, I'll spell it out for you. I . . . caused . . . Dad's . . . SCA."

Kurt's voice breaks up. I hear hiccupping and sniffling.

"No, no you didn't, Kurt."

"Yeah, I did. Stress can cause SCA. I stress Dad with my problems, and it will only hurt him more if I go out there."

Geez, Kurt may be right. Skipper needs help, and Kurt is too hooked on drugs to help anyone.

"Leave me alone, Valerie. If you hang around, I'll hurt you, too."

CLICK. Kurt cuts off the connection.

I grab a jacket and my car keys and drive over to Kurt's but can't get past security. He told them not to let me in.

When I get home, I find a voice message from Barbara stating, "You need to get Kurt out here."

Ch. 21 - Copping

KURT DOESN'T CALL and doesn't allow me into his gated complex. My voicemail pleas to talk with him get no response. I don't want to talk to anyone but Kurt, so I screen calls and don't answer the phone because, when it rings, it isn't Kurt's voice that I hear. I'm unable to eat. Food tastes like cardboard, and I spit it out. My stomach hurts but anxiety and uncertainty, not hunger, make me double over.

I have too much time on my hands at work. My boss is in New York representing the company at an iron and steel convention, and there's no work to do while he's gone. I need something to do but cannot latch on to anything worthwhile to occupy my mind. I need relief, too, and I don't want to wait for the end of the workday. There's no point in sitting at my desk feeling miserable, so I leave work without saying anything to anyone. I need to short-circuit my pain; I need a fix.

My hand is moist and trembles as I knock on the apartment door across from my own. Mitch cracks the door and looks out. "Hey, Valerie."

Unsure about how this is done, I say, "Kurt says he buys from you, and I'd like some."

Mitch looks me over, and I have trouble facing him. When I think he's about to turn me away, he opens the door. "Come on in." I cross the threshold into his apartment knowing that I shouldn't be there.

Two men sit on the couch, and no introductions are made. This is not a social situation. The men are buyers who have numerous scabs on their faces and arms. On one man's forearm, fluids ooze from a huge pus-filled lump. They are nervous or, more likely, strung out. Their eye movement is rapid indicating an inability to focus on any one object for long and reflecting tumultuous inner states.

Mitch's revolver, tucked in his waistband, signifies, "Don't mess with me." He motions me to a chair, and I push aside some newspaper debris before sitting.

The ashtrays on the tables are so full of cigarette butts that they need their own ashtrays. Empty food containers clutter the floor, and open beer and wine bottles are everywhere. Moaning sounds float down the hall into the living room like gruesome ghosts passing by. This apartment mirrors my own, so I know the groans come from either the bathroom or the bedroom.

When Mitch finishes his business and the two buyers leave, he turns to me. "Sorry 'bout the mess. Janet's not feeling up to cleaning. What'cha need?"

"A hit of heroin?"

Geez, I squeak out the words as if I'm unsure. Dammit, I *am* unsure.

"Mitch, I need a needle, too."

"All I have are used fits."

This isn't right. His needles are dirty.

"Valerie, you're a good kid. Why you want this?"

I'm angry. I hurt inside. I've been hurt. I'm lost. I miss Kurt. Nothing matters. My lips compress.

"Okay, kid." He pulls a small baggie from his pocket and takes a needle off the table. When he hands over the drug and syringe, he says, "Make sure to clean out this fit before using it."

As I hand him some cash, Janet enters the room. The whites of her eyes are yellow, her skin tone is jaundiced, and her movement is slow. She drops onto the couch and doesn't acknowledge my presence. She closes her eyes and moans.

I say goodbye, cross the hall, and enter my apartment. I get out some bleach and do my best to decontaminate the syringe, but my main concern at the moment isn't hygiene. I want relief and don't know what else to do or where else to turn.

It's my first time buying and preparing junk. It's my first time raising a vein to do my own injection. I'm scared, scared of myself and where I'm heading. I never thought I'd miss work to do drugs and never thought

I'd inject myself like a real junkie does. My hand shakes too much for me to insert the needle easily, but instead of waiting until I'm calmer, I jab the needle in, push on the plunger, and wait.

Damn, I don't feel anything.

Did Mitch rip me off?

Maybe I missed the vein and skin- or muscle-popped the heroin so it's coming on slowly, too slowly for me to feel a rush of relief. The only rush I get is the quick realization that I may have plunged into a lifestyle that I don't want.

Ch. 22 – The Face in the Abyss

I'M BREATHING TOO RAPIDLY to be high from smack. I should be nodding out and dropping into a euphoric stupor. Instead, my mind fires off self-accusatory statements about this self-destructive act. I know enough about the addict's life to understand what my future holds if I don't stop. If I continue scoring drugs and running them up my arm, what I've seen about addicts and drug use during the past few months will become my future. Those thoughts thread through my mind encasing me as effectively as spider-silk threads wrap tight their victims.

Dread about what I'm becoming forces me to try to shake it off by pacing the length of my apartment like a trapped animal. I stride along the walls in the back room where I make a "C" formation around the bed before roaming into and down the hallway. I go past a mirror on the wall opposite the kitchen. I walk a wide arc in the dining area past the window seat where the word, "SKIP," appears. Then, I dart past the living room windows before returning to the hallway, going past the mirror, and re-entering the bedroom. There, I begin the unsightly pilgrimage again: a "C" formation around the bed, a hallway sprint past the mirror, an arc around the window seat with its "SKIP" word, a race through the living room, and a return to the bedroom. The terrifying path into addiction turns me into a caged beast searching for a way to escape, and I travel the same route through my apartment over and over as the hours pass.

My arms wrap and unwrap rapidly across my body. I must look like a bat furling and unfurling its wings as the creature enters into and emerges from its coma-like, upside-down sleep. However, my arm movements make me look chilled as if I'm trying to pound warmth back into a frigid body.

I struggle to remain in touch with the physical world, but my mind is weary from the struggle to live a better life and urges a full retreat into a dark, internal place. A catatonic-like solution to all my fears beckons as a safe haven if only I would let go. I'm standing on the edge of an abyss. Fog-like oblivion seeps up from its black depth and urges me to let go, jump in, tumble down, fall apart. The black hole promises a fix more permanent than heroin.

I have faced the darkness many times. It was dark when my father entered my bedroom. It was dark in the elementary school boiler room after the gym teacher got me in there to "play" with the custodian. As the victim of human predators, I have fought the darkness for a long time, but this self-injection has turned me into both victim and attacker.

Frightened by the proximity of internal demons, my breathing turns into labored intakes and fitful expulsions of air. Agonized wheezes punctuated by an occasional howl emerge from my haunted throat.

Someone knocks at my door and brings my mind into a shadowy focus. I sniffle and wipe my nose on the end of my shirt.

"Valerie, are you okay?"

It's Alice, the woman who gave me Bean, but I don't answer the door; I don't want her to see me. I don't want anyone to see me with all my inner fears and demons so exposed on my face, in my mannerisms, in the way I move. I quiet my labored breathing, slow my frantic pace, and call out, "Just a nightmare. I'm all right."

"You're sure?"

"Yeah. Going back to bed now. Bye."

"Okay . . . well . . . okay . . . bye, Valerie."

It's very late at night or maybe it's extremely early in the morning. I'm not sure which. I seem to be burning up and freezing at the same time. Maybe I shouldn't have sent Alice away. Who can I turn to?

I look up and catch my reflection in the hallway mirror. I stop moving. My hands smack against the wall on either side of the mirror as I turn to myself. I stare into wild eyes that plead with me to stay away from madness.

I usually avoid my reflection, but tonight a feral need drives me to look at myself. At first, all I see are two horror-ridden eyes above nostrils flared wide as they grapple with uneven breaths. My lips are clenched, unwilling to wheeze or howl out sounds that might attract more attention from someone like Alice. As I stare into the mirror, I see my face ready to admit defeat.

Then, something changes as I peer at my frightened face. I see a tiny hint of fire there. I stare deep into my terrified eyes to make sure that I really do detect a slim, fiery desire to live. Is a will to fight really there? I study myself, latch on to that faint sliver of internal light, and sense an underlying strength. Maybe I'm delusional and fooling myself with false hope, so I gaze a long time, assessing, making sure that I can rely on the vigor within me. Yes, there is an inner fierceness that doesn't want to give in to drug addiction or the madness of a catatonic abyss.

I back away from my reflection; I back away from the mirror; I back away from giving in to heroin; I back away from the abyss of madness. I won't follow Kurt's path into addiction, and I won't drop into madness, at least not tonight.

I see the street light outside my building as it filters in through my curtained windows. I hear the hum of the refrigerator, and I feel Bean's tail caress my leg as she walks by. The sight, the sound, the touch should converge to signify a hard-fought battle won, but the stakes are too high to believe this war is over. Only a fool would completely shake off and deny the terror created by getting to close to the edge of an abyss. In reality, I haven't yet backed off far enough to feel safe. Basically, I've been warned that the abyss waits for me, and it's close, too damn close. I'm scared, more frightened than I've ever been. I'm cornered and pinned against the ropes.

Heroin should have quelled my internal beasts, but tonight it did not do that. The heroin horror of copping from Mitch, doing the teeth-gritted pull on an elastic armband, pumping up a vein, and plunging in a needle all triggered a ghoulish night instead of sedated peace. IV drug use is a road I cannot easily travel. Kurt won't see me, and I'm stuck in a job that has turned boring. What's left for me if I can't get relief from drugs?

I return to walking through my apartment but without feeling animal-caged crazy. My breathing has slowed, and my heart rate has calmed. I'm no longer desperate for escape, but I'm on a thread-bare return ticket to sanity. I want, I need, a permanent fix, but the abyss? There must be some other solution.

"SKIP." I saw that word each time I passed the window seat. "Skip" repeatedly captured my attention during my frenzied flight. "Skip," the word that anchored me during my desperate path from the back bedroom to the front living room.

Skip? Skip, rather than walk? No, that can't be right.

Skip, as in omitting something? But omitting what?

Skip? Am I still on the verge of madness or a breakdown?

I pick up Bean, feel her purring vibrations against my chest, and return to the window seat where I saw the word, "Skip." I spot an unopened letter tossed there days, perhaps weeks, ago. It is partially covered by another piece of neglected mail. I free it and see not "Skip" but the full name, Skipper, in the upper, left-hand corner of the envelope. I tear the letter open and find an informational pamphlet for the speech club Skipper told me about when we sat on his San Diego balcony and talked about fears. I grab at Skipper's advice but not about the speech club. According to his friend, Barbara, Skipper encouraged Kurt to seek counseling for his drug problem, and I decide to follow that advice.

I'm sitting on a border wall that's close to a Humpty-Dumpty tumble into addiction or madness. I need help to move away from that wall, so I yank the phone book from a drawer and create a list of therapists in the area. I decide to make an appointment with the psychologist whose name is at the bottom of my alphabetized list, the therapist whose last name begins with the last letter of the alphabet.

Part III

THE VOYAGE of the best ship is a zigzag line of a hundred tacks.
See the line from a sufficient distance,
and it straightens itself to the average tendency.

Ralph Waldo Emerson, "Self-Reliance," 1841

Ch. 23 - Summer Solstice 2002

A SIGN IN THE WAITING ROOM indicates that Dr. Z is with a patient. I'm too nervous to sit and read one of the magazines posted sentinel-style on a nearby rack, so I plod over to a window reinforced by octagon-shaped wire mcsh.

The medical building in which Dr. Z has an office is situated on a ridge a few miles south of Lake Erie. A somber mood sends my gaze down to the street rather than up to the sky or out to the lake. The street, lined with tidy bungalows and well-tended lawns, suggests an amicable neighborhood. Walkways, bordered by colorful flower beds, greet homeowners and their guests. Several homes sit on double lots where vegetable gardens grow in the extra space. It's the third week in June, and I see that cool-season plants are giving way to more heat-tolerant varieties.

On the steps leading to one house, a dark-skinned man laces up a pair of inline skates. I am about to turn away, trudge to a chair, and dump myself down when the man bursts out to the street and swirls, arms extended, ready to fly. He travels a figure-eight path up and down the street between the curb on one side and parked cars on the other. Large sycamore trees shade sections of the road, and the young man travels from the darkened sections of the street into the lighter areas with grace. He increases his speed, reaches peak skating velocity, and darts to the center of the road where he shoots his arms over his head and twirls in place.

His inspirational performance liberates a host of questions in my mind. Why isn't the skater's soul weighted down by stress or trauma? If his soul had been so weighted, how had it freed itself? How long had it taken him to learn to skate like that? How many times did he fall and get back up while learning? What secrets underlie his exuberant display?

A door opens behind me as I stand fixated at the window, and a deep voice inquires, "Valerie?"

I'm still held captive by the skater who now glides up and down the street in long, confident strides. The doctor, standing a few feet in back of me, clears his throat so I turn from the window. Blinded by the transition from a sunlit street to the dim hallway behind the man, I see only a shadowy silhouette.

"Yes? Dr. Z?"

"Come this way." My eyes adjust to the indoor lighting as Dr. Z motions in the direction of his office.

I leave the waiting room, walk the short hall, and enter a room with floor-to-ceiling windows that provide a view of the lake. The mustard-colored visitor's chairs have their backs to the view, and I take a seat in one of them. Dr. Z positions himself in a leather executive's chair on the other side of his walnut desk. He wears a charcoal-grey suit, a black tie, and a pale-blue shirt. Dark hair and a neatly trimmed beard frame his tanned face. The conservative, dark attire contrasts with eyes that generate warmth and acceptance.

"Hello, Valerie."

Unsure about what to say, I give a slight nod rather than speak.

"Tell me a little about yourself."

It's difficult to begin speaking. My family had taught me not to discuss personal matters with strangers or, as my mother phrased it, "Don't air your dirty laundry in public."

"Like what?" Two curt, reluctant, and defensive words slip out of my mouth.

"You decide."

I look away from Dr. Z. and slouch down until my butt is near the edge of the seat and my head, neck, and shoulders rest near the top of the seatback.

Dr. Z prompts, "Tell me a little about what you do during the day."

"I work." Dr. Z allows a silent space to grow into an uncomfortable gap between us. My slouched posture puts a strain on the back of my neck so I use my fists to push myself upright in the chair. I cross my legs and my right foot, now off the floor, begins a quick jittery motion that taps on the back of the desk. If Dr. Z only wants to know about what I do during the day, I guess talking about work would be okay.

"While in college, I worked summers at a large corporation filling in for clerks and office assistants as they went on vacations. Last summer, the company hired a Dartmouth-trained lawyer and I was assigned to work for him temporarily. He liked my work, and I stayed on rather than return to school."

I do not tell Dr. Z that I was glad when the summer job turned permanent because I had dropped out of college feeling scared and out of place there.

Dr. Z waits a moment before offering quiet encouragement. "Go on."

After a brief hesitation, I say, "The job was interesting and challenging until the partnership my boss created opened a plant a couple of months ago. Now there's little to do." My voice shakes when I add, "I feel trapped in my job."

That last statement makes my throat clench as I dam up sobs that want to burst forth. My eyelids clamp shut to keep tears from spilling out. The dungeon in my mind has no jailer other than myself, and I have no idea how to unlock the cell door and talk about what troubles me.

"What are you thinking about, Valerie?" Dr. Z's voice is calm.

I sense that opening up and talking about what torments me would be like ripping its protective bandage off and revealing a gash so horrible that it would disgust anyone, even Dr. Z. If he saw the horrors within me, he would reject me, so I change topics.

"Dr. Z, I'm getting only four or five hours of sleep each night and that's making it hard to stay alert at work during the day." When no sympathetic response comes from the doctor, I demand, "I need something to help me sleep."

"When did it start, your trouble sleeping?"

I can't tell Dr. Z that my trouble sleeping began the night I shot up the powder I bought from Mitch so I say, "It started after breaking up with my boyfriend, Kurt." The statement is close enough to the truth to be an okay answer.

"Tell me about Kurt."

I tamp down my irritation over Dr. Z's barrage of questions. If I want to get a prescription for sleeping pills, I'll have to humor the man. "I met Kurt last New Year's Eve. He asked me out, and we dated until recently."

"What did you like about him?"

I spend a few moments thinking about my first two dates with Kurt. I remember watching the winter sun sparkle through ice and taking photographs at the garden center. Those and other pleasant memories make it easy to give Dr. Z an answer. "Kurt opened my eyes to so many things I missed out on in life."

I tell Dr. Z about our initial dates and then talk about traveling to San Diego with Kurt to meet his dad and then sail. My whole being feels alive when I tell Dr. Z about hiking in Zion and spending the night on Angel's Landing with Kurt.

I'm relaxed and enjoying the memories when Dr. Z asks, "Why did you and Kurt break up?"

My lips draw shut, and my eyes narrow. I withdraw the bridge that allowed some communication with Dr. Z and retreat into my mental fortress. I'm not up to jousting with the doctor who keeps finding chinks in my armor and getting near the anguish deep inside me.

Dr. Z catapults an accusation through my defenses, "You're looking sullen."

"So, what," I respond. I expect Dr. Z's probing assault to continue, but when he speaks, I hear kindness instead of attack.

"I care about you, Valerie."

His concern clashes against my expectations, and my face scrunches up as I fight back tears.

Dr. Z's nonthreatening tone of voice asks, "Why are you here, Valerie?"

Sobs pulse up from my dark core, and my throat tightens as I fight to keep them from surging out into the open. Three words form in the shadowy depths of my soul, and I punch the verbal trinity out one word at a time. "I . . . hurt . . . inside."

If I say more, I'll break down. Dr. Z waits. The quiet space he occupies, like torture, makes me want to talk, but I can't continue without ranting or raging.

Dr. Z finally speaks. "I can help you feel better, Valerie."

I know I need help but shy away from most people like a mistreated pet slinks from those who try to help it. I, like an abused animal, know not to trust.

Dr. Z continues, "I recommend you come in twice a week."

I wasn't expecting to meet so often and balk. "I got permission to leave work early for this appointment but can't get time off twice a week." That should get him to back down and ease up on me.

"As your doctor, I'll support a request for time off two afternoons a week."

"Okay," I concede to get him to stop his painful and unsettling questions, but I expect something in return. "What about some sleeping pills?"

"We'll talk about medication next time. Let's do Tuesdays and Fridays at 3:00."

I'm not convinced Dr. Z or anyone can help me, but if I return, maybe I'll get a prescription.

During the drive home from Dr. Z's office, I mull over my first therapy session. My mental state has dropped so far into a dark cave that I don't see any light indicating an opening or a way out. I feel despondent until I remember the man skating in the street outside Dr. Z's office. If that skater can live so exuberantly, maybe I can, too. I'm distracted by these thoughts and images as I enter my building and climb the stairs. When I reach the landing below my floor, I look up and see Kurt outside my apartment door. I hear Bean's meows calling from inside, and I stop before taking the final steps to my floor. "Kurt?"

He looks down to where I'm standing. "Hi, Valerie."

When I reach the third floor and get close to Kurt, I see his wrinkled clothes and smell the body odor of someone who hasn't bathed recently. He looks high. His eyes no longer shine but peer furtively from dark surrounding circles, and he doesn't smile. I'm torn between relief over seeing Kurt, anger about his abandoning me, and concern that he's getting deeper into his addiction.

"I was forced to leave the condo."

Kurt looks angry when he continues, "I've had to start living in my car, and no one cares."

Kurt fidgets and scratches at fresh needle marks on his arms. He closes his eyes, takes a deep breath, and pleads, "Can I stay with you for a few days? Not long, only until I find somewhere else to live?"

My feelings for Kurt, at least the Kurt I knew before his habit got out of control, tug at me. I want to help but hesitate knowing it's not a good idea right now when I'm struggling to stay drug-free.

"Look, I brought you Dad's camera, the one you used on our photoshoots. I'm sure Skipper would want you to have it."

The camera, now a bargaining chip, reminds me of Kurt's dad and his recent heart attack. I delay my decision about letting Kurt into my apartment by asking, "How is Skipper doing?"

The question sets Kurt off. "How's *Dad?* Don't you care about how *I'm* doing?"

Kurt's behavior scares me. I back away and bump into my neighbor's door. A few moments later, that door opens and Mitch says, "Hey, dudes, what's up?"

I yearn for the Kurt I knew when we first dated and wonder if I can help him if I let him stay with me, but I hesitate. Before I can say anything, Kurt pushes by me and enters Mitch's apartment. Mitch looks at me and shrugs before closing his door and leaving me alone in the hallway.

Bean is still calling from inside my apartment, so I unlock the door and reach for her. She purrs as I cuddle her close to me, and I begin to settle down from my encounters with Dr. Z and then with Kurt.

I need to talk to someone who can give good advice. Alice and John are too involved in the drug scene to be of help unless I want to cop from them. Aunt Cora and Uncle Pete give great advice but they do not know about my and Kurt's drug habits. Barbara, Skipper's level-headed friend, knows about Kurt's drug issues so I call her.

"Hi Barbara. Sorry I haven't returned your calls sooner."

"Valerie, it's so good to hear from you."

"How is Skipper?"

"He's still in a nursing home but improves a little each week. How are you?"

"Okay, I guess. I saw Kurt."

After a short pause, she asks, "How's he doing?"

"He's living in his car but looking for somewhere to stay."

Barbara lets out a long breath. "Skipper was obligated to complete the sale on the condo. We haven't heard from Kurt since the new owner took possession."

"I'm worried about him, Barbara."

"Valerie, be frank with me. Is Kurt's drug habit a problem?"

It feels disloyal to admit it, but I do. Maybe they can help him. "Yeah, Kurt's drug use is out of control."

Barbara sighs. "Things will get rough for Kurt unless he goes into treatment. A few days ago, we had to close the bank account and credit card he shared with Skipper. He overdrew one account and made too many cash advances on the other."

I ache for Kurt and wonder what he'll do.

"Are you sure this is the best way to deal with Kurt's addiction? He looks terrible."

"I know it sounds tough." Barbara pauses and sighs again. "We want to help Kurt without supporting his habit, but he needs to want our help."

I see the logic in what she says, but after seeing Kurt, it's not a comforting rationale.

"Valerie, I know our actions sound harsh, but Skipper told me how difficult Kurt got the last time his addiction took over. Kurt knows we will help him if he goes into treatment, but he's refusing Skipper's offer to pay for drug rehab."

I'm quiet as I think about what she's saying.

"Can I give you some advice?" Barbara doesn't wait for an answer. "Focus on your well-being, Valerie. When Kurt's caught up in his addiction, he hurts the people who care about him."

It's difficult to face what Barbara says. I don't want to believe that the man who encouraged my photography and piano playing, the man who cooked meals for me, and the man who made love to me could also hurt me.

"Valerie, are you still there? Did you hear what I said?"

"Yes, I heard you. This is very hard for me." The words escape before I realize how hard it must be for Barbara who is caring for Skipper and dealing with Kurt's drug problem. "I'm sorry, Barbara. That's such a selfish thing to say."

"No, it's not selfish, Valerie. Skipper and I are concerned about you, and we realize this is hard on you, too."

I'm struck by their concern and ability to care about me when they have their own serious problems. Their kindness, a strange and foreign blow, leaves me reeling in the ring like a boxer taken off guard. I have no idea how to accept Barbara's kindnesses as much as my whole being yearns for and needs them.

"Can you take care of yourself and let us worry about Kurt?"

"I'll try," is all I manage to say.

"You take care, dear. Bye for now."

After hanging up the phone, I try to think about Barbara's advice, but I'm exhausted from the day's events and drop on my bed without brushing my teeth or changing into pajamas. It's difficult to focus on myself as Skipper and Barbara advised me to do, but I squeeze my eyes shut and tighten my fists as I try. Something pulls me toward thoughts of sailing with Skipper and my tension releases. I drift off and dream about a young man who flies with roller skates strapped to his feet.

Ch. 24 - Coming Clean and Getting Cleaned Out

DR. Z PREEMPTS MY PLAN to insist on some sleeping pills by speaking first at our second session. Without any greeting or a preamble, he says, "Last time, you mentioned how Kurt opened your eyes to things you missed out on. Tell me more about what you missed."

My head drops and my shoulders slump as I reflect on my unpleasant childhood. It was a time when I fantasized about escape. At bedtime, I told myself a story about a little girl trapped by a mean mother and father. She had a palomino pony that helped her flee by kicking through locked doors or leaping prison-like walls with her on its back.

I adored the parents on television's *Family Ties,* wanted to be one of the children in the family, and plotted how to mail myself to their address. I thought about the type of shipping crate that would allow air during transport. I planned the type of food I would need for the trip and how much water to take. What I didn't know was how much postage I needed, so I asked the postman. I still remember how his eyebrows shot up and pressed together when I asked him. Rather than answer what I thought was an excellent question for a postal worker, he just shook his head.

I was an unhappy child stuck in a family situation that was bad enough for me to want to live elsewhere. I wasn't able to escape until I became an adult, took my current fulltime job, and could afford an apartment. Escape from my dysfunctional family was one thing but being adrift in life as a young adult with few life skills left me needy and vulnerable. I look at Dr. Z who is waiting patiently for an answer to what I missed in life and wonder if I can trust this man.

I hold my breath as I decide whether or not to speak, gasp in some air, and blurt, "Dad died last winter. He was an alcoholic, passed out drunk in the snow, and froze to death." The information doesn't connect to Dr. Z's question, but it allows me to avoid exposing my internal pain. It's the best start I can make.

Dr. Z takes notes and waits for me to continue.

"You know what? I'm glad he's dead!" Tension mounts in my body and my hands form fists as I try to let go of the torment I've held inside for so long.

"Dad hated me, and I hid in my room as much as I could when I was a kid to stay out of his way. I have a right to hate him for how he treated me." Adrenaline prepares me to defend myself for breaking the Ten Commandment about honoring parents. I glare at Dr. Z, but he doesn't look shocked about the state of my soul for violating such a huge religious dictate. His calm acceptance of my feelings gets through to me, and I relax.

I back away from the most painful emotions I'm feeling and say, "I could never talk with dad. He either ignored me or hurt me when I tried."

"How so?"

I decide on one example that won't stir up too much of my anger. "In elementary school, my teacher once discussed social pleasantries and being polite. She gave an example about saying, 'What a lovely day,' when greeting someone. When I tried that greeting on dad one morning, he snarled back, 'What's so damn lovely about it!"

"How did that make you feel?"

"I got frightened and retreated to my room. I also began questioning everything the teachers told me. They didn't warn me or lead me to expect the reaction I got. What I learned in school often ran counter to what happened in my family, and that made it hard to believe teachers. They often said to rely on an adult for help, for example, but the adults in my home either ignored me or hurt me instead of providing comfort and help."

Dr. Z remains nonjudgmental about what I'm saying so I feel safe enough to tell him more. I talk about getting slammed onto the floor instead of comforted when I cried as a toddler. I talk about being viciously taunted for liking dad's friend JP, a man who laughed and played with me. I mention the elementary school gym teacher who, along with the school's custodian, lured me into the boiler room. I relate a story about returning from church camp where I had a wonderful time, missed the activities and my new friends, and cried. Dad yelled, "If you don't quit crying, I'll take you back there and dump you off." As I talk, I realize that in each case, I shut up and shut down to avoid further harm.

Talking about childhood injuries releases some of the pain that got entombed along with the hurt feelings. I had learned not to cry, so I compress my lips into a stoic stopper to throttle any sound. Then, silent tears escape and weave their way down my face. I brush them off and grab several tissues from a box on the table next to my chair. An internal dam bursts, and tears flood out. I feel myself falling apart, and I get scared.

Frightened by this emotional breakdown, I let Dr. Z fade from my view. Although I'm gazing in his direction, he appears unclear as if I'm viewing him through a smudgy television screen that keeps narrowing until Dr. Z's blurred face retreats to the center of an out-of-focus tunnel of vision. My hearing shuts down, and Dr. Z's words seem far away like I'm underwater and he's speaking to me from the edge of the pool.

I'm shutting off from my surroundings. I tighten my muscles while digging fingernails into the flesh on my arm. My tensed muscles and the discomfort in my arm help me reconnect, and I pick up the scent of soil from the houseplant on the table next to the tissue box. The smell triggers a memory of Aunt Cora in flowery garden gloves. She and I had carried a pail of kitchen scraps outside.

"Why aren't we taking these table scraps to the garbage can?"

Aunt Cora chuckles in response to my question.

"What's so funny about a bunch of smelly, slimy apple peels, eggshells, and watermelon rinds?"

Aunt Cora puts the pail next to a slatted bin, lifts the lid, picks up a pitchfork, and stirs the contents before asking me to empty the pail of kitchen scraps on top. When she pulls a tray out from the bin's bottom, she exhumes former kitchen castaways that had percolated down and been transformed into life-giving soil. We grab fistfuls, bring them to our noses, and inhale sunshine and darkness, life and death, vibrancy and repose. Everything in the world seems to be present, right there in my aunt's garden. For a while, I want the ground to open up and swallow me Jonah-style so I can be reformatted into something as rich and vibrant as the composted soil. When I look at my Aunt, she smiles as if she knows what I am thinking, and she turns my shaky preteen summer solid again.

I relax my muscles and stop digging my fingernails into my arm. I look at Dr. Z.

"What just happened, Valerie?"

"I felt far away from you. I went somewhere else, I think. Maybe to my aunt's garden." I don't know how else to explain how my eyesight narrowed and became fuzzy while my hearing deadened the sounds around me.

"You looked thoughtful. Were you thinking about anything in particular?"

"I was thinking about my Aunt Cora." I sit up straight and look directly at Dr. Z, the man who said he cared about me.

"Tell me a little about your aunt."

"She's my mom's younger sister by ten years, and she's ten years older than I am."

I pause wondering whether or not to say more. There's something in my mom's family that doesn't get discussed.

"Go on."

"Well, my mom and aunt are so different. My aunt reaches out to life, has all sorts of interesting hobbies and friends, and loves trying new activities. Mom leads a very restricted life and is afraid to try new things. She lives by a rigid set of rules. Every Monday is meatloaf; every Saturday, spaghetti. Dust furniture on Wednesdays; vacuum on Fridays. It's my mother's version of step on a crack, and she watches every step she takes and stays within self-imposed lines. She has no real friends, and I don't feel close to her."

"What makes your mother and her sister so different?"

"Good question." Their difference has puzzled me and stems from some murky family event involving my grandfather. Mom says her sister is lucky that their father died when Cora was seven or eight but she won't say why. My aunt, though, thinks Mom was molested by him."

"How old was your mother when her dad died?"

"She must have been seventeen or eighteen."

"When was your mom born?"

I don't know the year my mom was born although I do know the day of the year she was born. "August 21," is all I can tell Dr. Z.

"How old is your mom now?"

"I don't know. I don't know my parents' birth years by heart and don't know their ages. Well, I put 51 years old when I wrote dad's obituary so he must have been born in 1950 or '51."

"When is their wedding anniversary?" Dr. Z asks.

"I don't know." Dr. Z is quiet and provides the space in which I begin to understand somcthing. "It's like their marriage got erased by not celebrating its anniversary. It's also like their beings aren't worth celebrating with family birthday parties."

I reason this out a bit more and add, "You know, I feel erased somehow. My parents seemed happiest when I stayed away from them in my room. Mom even erased my physical connection to her whenever someone pointed out how much we looked alike. At those times, she insisted that I looked much more like my dad. It made me feel . . . well, erased. I can't think of a better word."

"That's a good observation, Valerie."

The impact of feeling erased in a family that consisted of strangers who never took root in each other's lives is immediate and troubling. We were never there for each other. Certainly, my parents were never there for me. It's a lot to think about, and I'm relieved when I look at my watch and see my time is almost up.

"Are you sleeping better?"

I shake my head.

"I'm prescribing an antianxiety medication. It might take a few weeks to take effect, but it could help you feel better and sleep more."

Back in my apartment, I distract myself from thinking about my family by organizing my clothes closet. When I discover Kurt's hoodie hanging there, I hug it close and realize how much I miss him. I don't need or want this reminder of Kurt in my unit, so I grab the hoodie and head across the hall to Janet and Mitch's apartment. Instead of doing a task at home, I'll leave the sweatshirt off with my neighbors and go out to fill my prescription.

When I knock, Mitch cracks the door open and wipes his nose on his sleeve. "Hey, Valerie."

"Can I leave this with you? It's Kurt's."

"Don't know when I'll see him." Mitch pauses as he sniffs and uses his hand to wipe snot from his nose. "But yeah, sure, leave it." When Mitch opens the door wider, I see Kurt's camera, the one he said I could have.

"Oh, I see his camera. I'm sure he'll be back for that."

"Uh, . . . no. He traded it for drugs."

It's the camera Kurt said he wanted to give me. Kurt lied and his betrayal drives home Barbara's warning that I could get hurt. I feel sick and need to get away from Mitch, so I push Kurt's hoodie at him, turn, and start down the stairs.

"See ya, Valerie."

I wave goodbye without turning back to Mitch. I hope the hand gesture means goodbye and not "see ya." If I see Mitch again, I might cop some dope to settle my unease.

Twice-a-week meetings with Dr. Z occur in quick succession.

"Last time, we talked about your family. Tell me a little more about your mother." I just sat down. Dr. Z doesn't waste time getting down to business.

"She's critical of everything I do."

"How so?"

"If she asks me to put something in a bowl for dinner, I never use the right bowl. If I help her by heating a can of vegetables, I never use the correct amount of heat. Nothing I do is good enough."

"How does that make you feel?"

"Angry. Definitely. I also feel unsure of everything I do and second guess each move. And, Mom never really talks with me. Whenever I have something important to say, she usually answers with some trite phrase that trivializes what I tell her. But, boy can she talk. I hate her phone calls because she goes on and on about all kinds of meaningless things like what she ate for breakfast or what she cleaned in the bathroom. I discovered Mom doesn't even know when I take the phone away from my ear and quit listening."

The announcement backs up into my ears, and I hear the underlying reality that either Mom doesn't care about me or she doesn't know how to care. Although she talks on and on and on, she never really connects with me.

"Dr. Z, she doesn't listen to me and has no idea what I'm going through."

"What doesn't she know?"

Whoa. To answer that question means talking about the fear that keeps me from going back to school. It would mean talking about what drives my self-destructive behaviors. I can't do it. My lips draw together in a tight formation as my teeth clamp together. I cross my arms across my chest and glare at Dr. Z daring him to breach my defenses.

In the silence and space that I'm given as Dr. Z waits, I struggle to reach out. I know I need to talk about these things, but the work is too hard.

Dr. Z asks, "Does anyone know what you're going through?"

I remember sitting with Skipper in San Diego when he asked what troubled me. If I could tell Skipper, maybe I can tell Dr. Z. "Kurt's dad, Skipper, knows a little."

"What did you tell him?"

"How afraid I am to go back to college." It's a weak start, but it's a beginning. I'm exhausted and ready to stop today's session.

"Why are you afraid?"

My heart pounds, and I want to leave. My arms unwind from my chest. My left hand grips the arm of the chair while my other hand forms a fist. "I'm terrified about speaking in class or giving presentations. There! You happy now?"

I pant, and my eyes dart back and forth. I expect an angry rebuttal to my outburst and get ready to defend myself.

Instead of anger, I hear Dr. Z say, "Valerie, I can help you."

I'm not convinced anyone can help me, but I need an ally. I take several deep breaths and open my fist.

Dr. Z continues, "If you could form a goal or two for our therapy sessions, what would you most like to accomplish?"

I sit back in my chair, and my heart rate slows.

"I want to go back to school."

I also need to deal with a very critical Mother who doesn't listen to me or meet my needs or help me in the ways I need help so I add, "And, I would like to talk with Mom without getting hurt or putting up with her lengthy monologues."

As I climb the stairs to my apartment, I look forward to getting some dinner and turning in early. Those thoughts get displaced by a noise coming from the third-floor hallway. When I reach that level, I see a man lying on the floor outside Mitch's apartment. Two teens are laughing as they wipe their sneakers in the man's hair.

I yell, "Stop it!"

Mitch opens his door to see what's going on as the teens quit their harassment and run down the stairs. When the man rolls over, I realize it's Kurt. He's high, and I don't think he knows or cares about what happened. Mitch shrugs and goes back into his apartment.

Kurt blinks and grins up at me. His slurred voice squeezes out, "I know you."

I open the door to my unit, toss my purse onto an end table, and help Kurt stumble into the entryway of my apartment. When I close the door, he teeters a moment before slumping down the wall. His clothes are rumpled and dirty. Dirt from the teenagers' shoes sticks to his greasy hair. His eyes, lidded and surrounded by dark circles, begin closing, and I leave him to sleep off whatever he ingested or injected.

I'm at the stove making something for us to eat when I hear Kurt begin to stir. I get a glass, fill it with tap water, and go to where Kurt is sprawled inside the entry door to my apartment. He sits up, takes the glass, and gulps down a couple of swallows between dry and cracked lips. His raspy voice asks, "Can I stay here tonight?"

When I hesitate, he adds, "Just for one night. I've got somewhere to go tomorrow."

Before I can answer him, I get distracted by long and persistent horn blasts from the driveway between my building and another three-story. I go to the window and see Kurt's SUV blocking the drive. The horn-honking comes from a tenant who needs to get by and into his or her parking spot.

"Where are your car keys? I need to move your vehicle."

Kurt looks puzzled and then searches through his pockets. The horn honking continues while Kurt locates the keys and hands them over. I dash into the hallway and run down the stairs. As I approach Kurt's SUV, the horn honking stops and a man leans out of his jeep, "What the hell, lady? You're damn lucky I ain't called the cops. Move that friggin' thing before I ram it down."

I tamp down my annoyance, ignore the angry driver, and fire up Kurt's SUV. After finding a parking space on the street, I look around Kurt's vehicle. There's a soiled sleeping bag on the back seat. Crumpled shirts, jeans, and boxer shorts are tossed everywhere. Kurt is obviously in deep trouble, and his circumstances tug at my heart. Maybe if I let him stay overnight, I can get him to take Skipper up on his offer to help with treatment. It's worth a try.

I gather up Kurt's clothes before leaving his vehicle and heading back to my apartment. I pull clean sheets and a pillow from the linen closet and place them on the couch. "You can sleep there tonight."

It's an awkward moment because we so recently shared a bed, but he doesn't complain or argue.

"Go take a shower while I do some laundry. There's a fresh bath towel on the rack. You can wear my robe while I wash your things."

When he hands over his clothes, I add them to the laundry from his car, grab some quarters and detergent, and leave for the basement laundry room. When I return, Kurt is out of the shower.

"That felt good. Thanks."

"How 'bout some dinner? It's not much, a little canned spaghetti sauce over noodles. You hungry?"

He nods.

I put a couple of plates of spaghetti on the table and sit down. Kurt takes a chair but doesn't look at me while we eat. I don't blame him for averting his eyes; he must know he looks bad.

"Have you been living in your car?"

The question rouses his anger. "Yeah, that bitch Barbara had me thrown out of Dad's condo."

"She had to go through with the sale Skipper started months ago."

Kurt glares in my direction and throws his fork down. "So, you're on her side!"

I push my chair away from the table. Kurt's irritation scares me, but I manage a calm, "Kurt, we are all concerned about you, and . . . "

"Yeah, right," he interrupts. "I wouldn't be in this state if you all cared so much!"

"Skipper wants to help. Please let him."

"I don't need help."

Kurt gets up and grabs the bottle of rum I keep in the cupboard. He returns to the table, sits, yanks out the cork, and drinks from the bottle. It's futile to talk with Kurt while he's drinking, so I leave him at the table, pick up a book, and head to the laundry room. As I pass John and Alice's apartment, the door flies open and Alice spots me. She stops, hesitates, then motions me to come in.

"How're you doing, Valerie?"

"Okay. I can't stay long. I need to get some clothes in the dryer. What's up?"

She points to the couch where a blanket covers a very large bulge. Alice doesn't look happy as she flips the blanket aside and reveals about 50 bricks of marijuana. After she drops the blanket back in place, she says, "Come on, Val, I'll help you with your washing."

We walk down the hall to the laundry room, remove Kurt's clothes from the washer, push them into a couple of dryers, and start the machines. Then, we hop onto the dryers and sit side-by-side.

"John bought all those bricks of weed without my knowledge. He spends the day breaking them up, weighing them, and putting them into plastic bags."

"So? I thought he always dealt."

"Yeah, he sold a little weed now and then for extra cash, but this . . . this is turning him . . . turning us, if I stay, into a major dealer. I didn't sign up for that when we married."

While the dryers hum beneath us, she complains that John doesn't want to go out anymore because he fears that someone will break in to steal the drugs or the cash. They can't put the drug money into a checking or savings account without taking a chance that the untaxed bills will draw attention from the government. She's also concerned about all the strangers who arrive in their apartment carrying guns. Word-of-mouth tips have enlarged their clientele base, but that means many strangers arrive at their door.

I have my own problems with Kurt and can't take on Alice's, so I try placating her. "I'm sure everything will be fine, Alice."

She nods but doesn't look convinced. "You know, when John and I met in the late 60s, I thought living a Bohemian lifestyle with him would be fun, so I turned my back on my well-to-do family and my business degree from Vassar. Now, I'm too old to find a different path in life, but I'm not sure I can stay with John if he keeps dealing so much."

The dryer buzzers go off, and Alice says, "Val, I'll help you fold."

"Thanks, Alice, but I'm okay."

"Well, all right. I needed to vent and knew you'd understand. Sorry to have dumped my problems on you. Mitch tells me you have your own troubles with Kurt."

Alice hugs me and leaves. I yank the clothes from the dryers, fold them, and return to my unit where Kurt lies on the couch with his back to me. I stack his clean clothes next to the couch and recork the not-quite-empty bottle of rum that's sitting on the floor. I pick up Bean and say goodnight, but Kurt doesn't answer. He's either asleep or ignoring me. In my bedroom, I check my wallet and am relieved to see my cash and credit card are still there. I make sure Mom's class ring and Dad's bayonet are still hidden safely in the linen closet. They are.

In the morning, Kurt remains asleep while I shower and dress for work.

"Kurt, wake up. You need to go, and I need to get to work."

He rolls over. "Aw, Val, come on. Can't I sleep a little longer and let myself out?"

I know it's a bad idea to let him stay.

"All I need are a few hours before I meet my new roommate. What's the harm in letting me stay a little longer?"

I'll be late for the office if I hang around, and I do not have time to force Kurt out if he refuses to leave.

"Okay, Kurt. Do me a favor, though."
"Sure, what?"
"Call your dad."
Kurt turns away.

When I return in the evening, I don't see Kurt's SUV parked on the street. I'm relieved that he's gone but that feeling of relief turns into dismay when I approach my apartment door. Two pawn tickets rest in the crack between my door and the frame around it. When I enter, I see that Kurt and his clean clothes are gone, but so are my television and stereo.

I should be angry, but anger is too simple an emotion for what rises up within me. There's no denying that I am overwhelmed by sadness and hurt. A physical sensation creeps into my core, a pain that makes me double over, arms wrapped around my stomach. At first, I take shallow, quick breaths, but they soon turn into deep in-breaths and slow out-breaths. I get mental flashes of who I am because of Kurt. He may have stolen from me and lied to me, and he may be gone from my life, too, but he left me with the ability to see and photograph the magic in the world around me. His encouragement when I learned piano opened up my emotional life. He introduced me to the inspiring impact of sailing and traveling to places like Zion.

I carry the best parts of Kurt, now firmly entwined in my personality. Those new parts of my makeup are valuable, and I resolve to protect them. I'll heed the advice from Skipper and Barbara by taking care of myself. I decide to move away from John, Alice, Mitch, and Janet. It won't be easy, but I'll do my best to get away from Kurt and his drugs, too.

Ch. 25 - Set and Setting

"YOU'RE LOOKING SULLEN," Dr. Z says when I enter his office, and I dislike the comment. Although his assessment of my mood is accurate, it's an unfair one. It hasn't been easy making arrangements to move after Kurt ripped me off. I spent the weekend looking for somewhere else to live. I spend every spare minute scrounging around for moving boxes, packing, and getting ready to move. I've been drinking more than usual to help me sleep, but I toss in bed anyway for most of the night. I'm tired and irritable. If I am looking sullen, as Dr. Z points out, I have good reason to be.

"No shit," I tell Dr. Z. "Life ain't easy, and times are tough."

In the silence following my outburst, Dr. Z shows no hint of striking back. "What's going on?"

"Someone broke into my apartment and stole my TV and stereo." I'm looking at my lap as I talk and suspect Dr. Z knows I'm not quite telling the truth.

"Do you feel safe there, after the break-in?"

"I need to move. Over the weekend I found a nice, two-bedroom single-wide for rent. The mobile-home park in which it sits looks well-managed, so I decided to take it. I'll lose a deposit for breaking my current lease, but I need to get out of that building."

"Sounds like you're protecting yourself and making good choices. Is there anything else you want to tell me about your move?"

I shake my head. I'm too embarrassed to talk about Kurt and what he did.

"Last time, we discussed two goals. One is returning to college, and another is communicating better with your mother."

I'm relieved that Dr. Z isn't prying into the details of why I'm moving.

"Does your mother know you're in therapy?"

"No. I haven't visited Mom for some time and avoid talking with her by phone. I haven't even told her sister, my aunt, about this. So, no, she doesn't know."

"I want to invite your mom to attend some sessions with you to talk about your needs and how she can help. Would you be okay if I asked her to come in?"

"What will you say if she demands to know why I'm seeing you?"

"I won't share anything you don't want me to. I'll tell her you're under my care and ask her to join us during some of your office visits."

"I bet she'll refuse to come in."

"Okay. Let's assume she won't join you in therapy when I ask her. How might you tell her about your needs?"

"Well, I'd call her instead of facing her in a visit. If I break through all her chatter, she would criticize me for being afraid of returning to school. She would say my fears are nonsense, and I need to get over them. You know, 'pull myself up by my bootstraps.' Then, she would launch into one of her monologues filled with trivial matters. She won't listen."

"Okay. What would happen if you phoned and told her you have something important to talk about but need to leave for an appointment in 20 minutes?"

"She'd blow up about my only having 20 minutes for her."

"If she ignores your need and blows up, remind her it's important for her to listen to you."

"What happens if she won't listen and the 20 minutes go past?"

"Tell her you're sorry you didn't get a chance to talk about what you wanted to tell her, you need to go, and you'll call another time. Then, tell her goodbye and hang up."

"It seems so simple and logical to have a goal for the conversation and set time limits. Why couldn't I come up with that solution?"

"You and your mother have a long history of conversations that are now habits. Long-term patterns get entrenched and are difficult to see clearly let alone change."

I'm excited about trying out Dr. Z's advice.

He comments, "You're smiling."

I am no longer staring at my lap in embarrassment over my lies to Dr. Z about Kurt. I spend the remainder of my session venting about how difficult my days are balancing work, therapy, and the move.

Just before my hour with Dr. Z ends, he asks, "Valerie, before you go, do I have permission to call your mother about joining us?

I'm not sure I want Mom in therapy with me but I nod, "Okay, Dr. Z."

I haven't yet talked with Dr. Z about my drug use and decide to ask Uncle Pete about my dad's heroin problem. I still get drug cravings, and want to learn how Dad quit drugs after he returned from Vietnam.

When I dial my aunt and uncle's home, Uncle Pete answers. "Hey, Valerie. I'm afraid you missed Cora; she just left with a friend to go shopping."

"That's okay. I want to talk with you."

"What's up, sweetie?"

"At dad's wake, you mentioned that some of the Vietnam veterans who used heroin during combat were able to quit without treatment when they returned from the war. Can you tell me more about that?"

I'm nervous but know Uncle Pete is good at answering questions without asking questions. Still, he's no dummy, and I'm sure he wonders why I want more information.

"Well, okay. When I did some volunteer work at the VA, I heard a psychoanalyst discuss what he called drug, set, and setting. Hmm, come to think of it, that doctor wrote a book with the title, *Drug, Set, and Setting*."

"What did he mean by set and setting?"

"Set is the user's personality profile. Some people are more prone to using alcohol or drugs when they get stressed or when something traumatic happens to them."

"So, there was something about Dad, his family history, and his survivor's guilt that fed his need to self-medicate. As a result, drugs and alcohol appealed to him more than they would to someone who didn't have those factors going on."

"Yes, but it's not only personal issues that make a difference in drug habits. Everyone experiences stress, but many people manage without turning to drugs because they have learned better coping skills."

"Okay, let's see if I got this right. Some people have better life skills, like anger management, or learn skills that provide alternatives to using alcohol or dope."

"Good. You got it, Valerie. As for the setting, that has to do with social and cultural factors. Today, there are many ways drinking gets managed culturally and socially. 'Friends don't let friends drive drunk,' would be one example. In the 60s, hippies encouraged the use of LSD with the phrase, 'turn on, tune in, and drop out.' Such factors facilitate or discourage drinking or drug use."

"I get it, Uncle Pete. When drug-using Vietnam veterans went home where people didn't use heroin, that setting formed a brake on their use."

"Yes, exactly."

I hear Uncle Pete breathe in and know he has more to say. He loves talking about theoretical issues and his voice quickens. "You know, the setting shouldn't surprise anyone when you think about it. Over time, the environment shapes many creatures."

I'd better get Uncle Pete back on track before he changes the topic to evolution. "Yes, that's very true, but what about drug use?" I smile wondering if I just shaped Uncle Pete's speech.

"Oh, yes. Don't forget the drug part. How often one uses, how large a dose it is, how much gets ingested, and how potent the drug is all combine to make it easier or harder to quit."

It must be much harder for Kurt to quit than it is for me given his long history with powerful drugs. I kept most of my narcotics use to weekends and was a passive user in the sense that I let Kurt buy the drugs and inject me except for the last time I used. Uncle Pete interjects, "Valerie, your mom called awhile back all in a state saying you won't talk with her. Anything you want to tell me?"

"Uncle Pete, I'm trying to work out a few things, that's all. Tell you what, I'll call Mom soon."

"Is there anything your aunt and I can do?"

"Thanks, Uncle Pete, but I'm okay." I don't tell him about my upcoming move, my change of setting, one that will take me away from the dealers and users in my former apartment building.

"We're on your side. You know that, right sweetie?" Uncle Pete must suspect something isn't quite right.

"I do, Uncle Pete, and I appreciate it more than you know."

After I hang up, I decide to destroy my contact information for dealers and get a new phone number for myself. I can't leave any forwarding information with Alice and John unless I want to take a chance that Kurt will get my new address and show up. Making a complete break isn't easy, but I have to do it or there would be no point in moving and changing settings.

Kurt, of course, knows my work number, but he hasn't called me at work since his father's heart attack. At least he hasn't yet called me there. I can't change my phone number at work, but I can ask security not to allow Kurt access to the company if he should show up. It hurts to make this break with him, but I can't take a chance on facing myself in the mirror again if I start careening toward drug use. I'm not sure I can stay drug-free if I see Kurt again.

Two days later, I get a call from Mom. She's not happy about Dr. Z asking her to come into therapy, and she's frightened by my discussing family problems with an outsider.

"Never air your dirty laundry in public, Valerie! I've told you that over and over and over," she shrieks. "What are you telling that man?"

"He's my doctor, Mom."

She ignores that comment and begins blabbing about how inconsiderate I am to put her through this. When she launches into a monologue about what she bought at the grocery store and what she cleaned, I do not go silent and fuzz out like I usually do. Instead, I try interrupting her, but she doesn't hear my feeble attempt. Finally, I focus on what Dr. Z urged me to do.

"Mom, you're not listening to me. What I want to tell you is very important. My therapist thinks you can help me by coming in to some of my sessions."

"Talking never helped anyone. Anyway, I'm selling the house and leaving to go back to West Virginia. I can't visit some idiot shrink!"

At this point, mom talks about what she is packing into boxes for her move. She doesn't know I'm packing for my move.

"Mom, I have to go soon; I'm boiling noodles and need to drain them in five minutes."

I'm not cooking, but I follow Dr. Z's advice about cutting her conversations short when she doesn't respond to my needs. It works. She says, "Oh, dear, you'd better go before you overcook the pasta. Better safe than sorry, you know."

"Bye, mom."

I'm smiling as I hug Bean. Is it that easy to stop a one-sided telephone conversation?

Although Dr. Z thinks it's a good idea to have Mother join me in therapy, I'm not sorry that Mom refused to comply with his request. I need to be on my own and away from family to sort things out. I can't trust Mom's influence because I am sure she doesn't know how to help me. She might inadvertently continue to hurt me instead. I need to find my way without her help.

A day later, when Dr. Z discusses Mom's refusal to enter therapy with me, I'm pierced by a painful realization.

"Valerie, I usually refuse to treat a patient when a parent won't attend. Most parents who initially refuse will comply if it means their child won't get treatment. In your case, I'm going to make an exception."

"I'm not surprised about Mom's refusal to come in. My parents rarely helped me with anything. I've learned to rely on myself and not ask for much from my family."

My eyes dart back and forth while I sit motionlessly and take quick breaths of air.

"What are you thinking, Valerie?"

A fault line in my mind opens to release a dark thought into awareness. "I thought all parents refused to help their children. I thought that was normal."

As it dawns on me that most parents must love, or at least like, their children and do what they can to help them, I realize how devastating my childhood was. My chin trembles, and I have difficulty breathing as I try not to cry. In a quiet voice, I ask Dr. Z, "It isn't normal, is it? I'm in deep trouble, and can't get help from my mom. Most parents would help, wouldn't they?"

I collapse into sobs that cut through me in a painful yet strangely healing manner. I double over in profound grief over the losses I suffered because of my terrible childhood. Howls push up from a knotted place deep within me. They cut through my throat, a throat that can no longer thrust them back inside, and they hurl themselves out of my mouth in convulsive, vomited blasts. As painful as the expulsion of my sobs and howls is, I sense that this powerful grieving also has a cleansing impact.

When my sobbing subsides, I resolve not to be in contact with Mom more than necessary. I will not hurt her on purpose, but I will do what's best for me even if that means she will feel hurt as I protect myself.

Ch. 26 - Filling (or Falling Into) the Void

"I AWAKE FEELING SCARED," I tell Dr. Z. "Then, I fuzz out or enter a fugue state. I'm not sure what happens during that time but hours pass as if they are only minutes. When I return to awareness of the world around me, I get an urge to do drugs."

I've been in therapy for about one month and have decided to introduce Dr. Z to my drug issue.

"Tell me more about the drugs," Dr. Z says.

It's not easy to talk about my drug use, but I need help with staying clean. "I started using drugs when I began dating Kurt. The drugs helped me feel better whenever I became nervous or troubled by something. Now that I no longer see Kurt and don't live in a building with drug dealers, I'm not using, but I do think about drugs whenever I'm scared."

"What makes you anxious or scared?"

"Geez, just about everything. Before I met Kurt, I held all my bad feelings in check but felt cold inside. I sort of watched life around me like it was on television or something. I first discovered that marijuana made me feel at ease and stay connected to those around me when I smoked at a New Year's Eve party. That's when I met Kurt."

I consider how dating Kurt, learning photography from him, playing his piano, and using LSD opened me up. I tell Dr. Z, "When I began using drugs, they amplified the good things I experienced with Kurt and made me feel less frozen or afraid."

"It sounds like Kurt and his drugs helped you connect to positive emotions."

"Yeah, . . . yeah, that sounds right. But there were other times when drugs cut me off from emotions I didn't want to feel."

"Tell me more about those other times."

"Okay. Well, two occasions stand out. One occurred when I felt guilty over dad's death and another happened when I couldn't face mom's demand to live with her and go back to school. I asked Kurt to give me some strong drugs both times, and narcotics stopped me from having to face the unpleasant emotions I was going through."

"You mentioned taking marijuana and LSD. Did you use anything besides those two drugs?"

An audible puff of air escapes through my lips, and I look away from Dr. Z. "Powders. Junk." I manage only a whisper when I reveal that.

"How did you do the powders? Snort or inject them?"

I cannot face Dr. Z. It's difficult to admit I used drugs intravenously. I fear he will think of me as some sort of lowlife, so I avoid a more direct answer.

"I didn't mix it with weed and smoke it."

"Does that mean you snorted or injected heroin?"

Dr. Z's tone of voice is neutral, free of judgment or negativity, so I say, "I let Kurt inject me."

The admission is a relief. I need help staying clean and trust that Dr. Z can help me. I don't want to slide back into using because I know the downside of drugs too well. I think about missing work, getting shot and having friends operate, passing out and being on the verge of death, coming down with Hepatitis C (a harsh liver disease), stealing from friends and lovers, pawning stolen goods or trading them for drugs, and standing at the edge of madness.

I face Dr. Z and say, "I've stopped using, but I think about doing drugs every day. I'm at a loss as to how to live without narcotics. I don't know how people find pleasure in normal activities, and I don't know how to fill the void in my life, the void left by Kurt and his drugs."

My head goes down, and I lower my eyes. "I can even sense a needle going into my arm when I have an urge to use."

"Okay, let's try replacing an unwanted thought with something else. Whenever you think about using drugs, replace that thought with a different one, one you find desirable."

"Like what?"

"Describe a time you felt happy."

I tell Dr. Z about being in Zion National Park.

"You could think about that park whenever you feel an urge to do drugs."

"Yeah, . . . yeah, I can try that."

"Visualize yourself in Zion right now."

When I try, however, I do not think about Zion. Instead, I think about sailing and can even feel the wind and waves around me as I picture myself on Skipper's boat.

"You're smiling."

"Yeah," I say as my face brightens. "I began thinking about sailing instead of hiking at Zion and started to feel the motions of being on a boat."

"Good. Keep that technique in mind whenever you feel an urge to do drugs. Think about sailing instead."

"I'll work on that."

"As far as finding something to fill the void, you talked about photography and said you bought a camera."

"Yeah, I did buy a camera, a used one."

"What do you enjoy about photography?"

I tell Dr. Z about the times Kurt and I took photographs. I tell him about seeing the sunrise through icicles and discovering how Kurt viewed the world when I saw his photographs from the garden center.

"Maybe photography can help fill the void and be an enjoyable, normal activity."

I know that is a great idea. Doing it in place of moping around won't be easy, but I've got to try.

"Dr. Z, you know what? I'm going to take my camera and go on some organized hikes at the city's Metroparks. I have a calendar of park events, and I'll see if there are any hikes for this weekend."

"Good," says Dr. Z. I suspect we both know that this positive-sounding step will take resolve and courage on my part to actually accomplish.

The county's 20,000-acre Metroparks system of nature centers, beaches, marinas, and greenspaces provides hiking trails, multipurpose paved routes, and bridal paths. Park rangers conduct programs geared to each season. I select two hikes from the park's calendar and load film into my garage-sale-cheap Nikkormat, one of Nikon's lower-end cameras. The camera is an old-style SLR or single-lens-reflex and has only one automatic feature – the light meter. I manually set the aperture opening, adjust the shutter speed, and turn the focusing ring. It's a heavy piece of equipment especially when I attach the telephoto lens, but I'm happy to have it.

The first park event I attend is a tallgrass prairie hike on a sunny Saturday afternoon. I arrive in time to hear a park ranger greet a group of attendees, mostly women and a few children or grandchildren, at a nature center. I join the group, and we follow the ranger into a four-acre meadow. The ranger names the prairie plants and describes each plant's unique identifying features. As the ranger talks, the field transforms from a bunch of green stems with leaves and flowers to a field of individual plants. The black-eyed Susan, grey-headed coneflower, cup plant, tall coreopsis and prairie dock have yellow blossoms. Punctuating this lemon-colored display are the purple coneflower's majestic hue, the wild bergamot's lavender offering, and the royal catch fly's star-shaped bursts of red. I do my best to photograph the individual prairie plants against a background of puffy, white clouds.

When the hike leader circles back to the visitor center, one of the women in the group stops near a tree and motions me to join her. She's staring at something.

I approach, but stop when she says, "It's a nymph."

The woman sounds batty. I give her a puzzled look and begin to leave when she continues, "It's a cicada nymph, and it's hatching."

I walk to the tree and see a bulge with wings and large eyes issuing from a brown shell.

The woman is excited. "It's rare to see this. Typically, cicada hatchings occur at night when their predators aren't out."

It's an amazing, transformative birth to watch, and I photograph the cicada as it emerges from its shell. It cannot move after it frees itself from the old casing because its wings, upon hatching, are too wet for flight. It's a vulnerable time for this insect.

The woman whispers, "Before it can fly, its wings dry and pump up somehow."

Soon, the wings elongate and separate from the body. The adult form is ready for flight, and it takes off.

"Wow," we say in unison.

"Hi. I'm Georgene."

"Valerie."

We walk back to the nature center and talk about wildlife. Georgene knows a lot about plants, trees, birds, and insects and loves it when the outdoors reveals its intricacies to her as it did with the cicada.

I notice a ring on her finger. "Are you married?"

"No, but most people think I am because of the ring."

"Why do you wear it then?"

"I don't think of it as a wedding band. This ring doesn't symbolize being true to another, but it reminds me to be true to myself. It also helps avoid unwanted attention from men. I'll do the choosing when it comes to dates."

"What type of man are you looking for?"

She laughs and her eyes sparkle. "A man who would give me a bouquet of wildflowers rather than sanitized ones from the florist."

"But a wild bouquet might have spiders!"

"Yes, exactly," she says as her eyes take on a mischievous glow. "It might harbor thorns and cobwebs, too, but it would represent life from its most beautiful to its more difficult. I don't want a dozen showy roses with thorns snipped off."

She beams my way, and I'm curious to know more about her. "Do you work?"

"I'm an accountant for a local firm. What do you do?"

"I'm just an administrative assistant," I mumble feeling inferior to her because of my job. She probably has her own assistant to boss around, and I look away from her in embarrassment.

She places a hand on my shoulder. "It's a pleasure to meet you, Valerie."

Her kindness gets through to me, but she reminds me of the aspirations I abandoned when I dropped out of college. I experience a bittersweet mix of pleasure from her company and sadness because of the reminder about my failure. That mix of happiness and regret makes me uncomfortable enough to be relieved when Georgene says, "Gotta run. I hope to meet up with you on another hike, Valerie."

The next day, Sunday, I join Ranger Hal as he leads a group across a creek, up a steep embankment, and along a ridge overlooking the stream we crossed. The group is larger and more diverse than the one that met yesterday for the prairie walk. There are as many men as women and a greater range in ages. I remain at the back of the line of hikers where I'm less visible and less vulnerable. Ranger Hal stops at a promontory, looks at me in the back with my camera raised for a photo, and says, "Photographers belong in the front."

What? My body enters flight mode. My mind tells me it's not safe in front of a group of strangers, and it's very unsafe to be the focus of attention.

The group creates an opening for me to pass. I would rather run but do not see any way out of the situation. Dr. Z once said he can't tell when my heart is racing from anxiety. To use his words, "I always look like the picture of composure," so I embrace his statement about my tranquil appearance as I walk to the front. I may look serene, but inside I feel frozen as I move ghostlike and silent through the group. I'm aware of eyes looking at me and distract myself from the unwanted attention by tightening a fist and concentrating on my flexed arm muscles rather than on the people around me.

In order to evade facing the group, I do not turn around when I reach Ranger Hal at the head of the pack. Instead, I kneel with my back to everyone and take a few photographs from the edge of the ridge we are on. I remain crouched, enjoying the view as Ranger Hal explains how the river valley formed and how the blue-grey siltstone we are standing on was quarried in the late 1800s for sidewalks, porch stoops, foundations, and even laundry-tub basins. I concentrate on deep breathing and relax enough to realize the ranger reminds me of JP, the man who played with me when I was a child, the man from whom I had to distance myself when our relationship angered Dad. I'm about to smile when Hal is ready to move on and says, "If our photographer falls off the cliff, just grab her camera strap."

It's too much attention. I begin shaking as Hal returns through the crowd to lead them to another overlook. At least the change in direction puts me at the end of the group again, but the attention from Ranger Hal triggers a flashback. I panic. No one notices when I stop walking with the group and slip away. My mouth gapes fishlike to take in gulps of air. My midsection tightens around knots of pain and nausea. Sweat dampens my hairline and turns my clothes into a clammy layer.

I half stumble, half slide, down a slope made of loose pieces of shale and splash through the creek at the bottom before scurrying for the safety of my car. My unsteady hands drop the car keys three times before I get the door open. I get in the back seat, remove the camera from my neck, wrap my arms around my midsection, and curl into a fetal position. My face tightens and my eyelids clamp shut. No specific memories flash up, but powerful dark emotions pulse through me. All I can do is ride out the waves of panic.

When my mental storm abates, it leaves behind a shipwreck of broken-up, negative thoughts. I tell myself I'm not worthy of positive attention or relationships with people like Georgene or Ranger Hal. There's no point in fighting for anything better. I am not worth it. My mind flounders for something to keep me afloat.

I unfurl my body from its defensive posture and climb into the front seat determined to feel better. I know where to go. I know what I need.

The engine starts, and the car leaves the park as if I'm not in charge of the vehicle or its movement. I'm on autopilot homing my way to Mitch and Janet's to make a buy. My tongue rolls across my lips in anticipation of relief. Damn the traffic and traffic lights that slow my flight to cop drugs. The slow drive, however, allows enough time for competing thoughts to seep into awareness, and those thoughts begin to cool my urge to cop drugs.

My old apartment building looms next to the curb where I've stopped although I don't remember pulling over and parking. My body shakes but not from anticipation. I know this isn't what I should do. My wrists hit the steering wheel over and over until my fists find my face where they pummel my forehead. I do not get out of the car. A couple of minutes pass before I settle back into the seat, put my hands in my lap, and let my breathing become regular. My eyesight goes from autopilot awareness to an ability to mindfully look around. Dr. Z said I should call him if I get close to using narcotics.

I drive to a safe place away from my former apartment building to make the call. At first, I get Dr. Z's answering service. When I tell them it's an emergency, they put me through to the doctor.

"You said I should call you if I get close to using drugs. I drove to a dealer's place but didn't cop. I want to give up on myself."

"What happened?"

I tell Dr. Z about meeting Georgene on one hike and then being the center of attention in Ranger Hal's hike.

"Did anyone hurt you?"

My mind fights off the fear of being hurt so I can find the truth. "No, no one hurt me. They were nice to me."

"Valerie, are you still going to cop?"

I am safer and calmer. "No. At least not today."

"You took on more than you're ready for. That's all that happened."

Damn it. I'm angry. "Why is life so difficult? Why can't I enjoy what other people enjoy without wanting to do drugs?"

"You'll get there, Valerie. Let's concentrate on one thing at a time and focus on getting your mind off drugs. Can you do that?"

The urge to inject a narcotic remains although I don't intend to buy, so I close my eyes and visualize being aboard a sailboat as it heels away from the wind. I sense getting lifted into the air with my hand on the tiller while I listen to waves hit the bow.

"I'm not going to use, Dr. Z, not today."

Ch. 27 - Kittens and Kids

MY INSOMNIA INTENSIFIES AFTER the hikes where I met Georgene and caught the attention of Ranger Hal. I won't be joining ranger-led park events this weekend. Instead, I gulp down some coffee, grab an energy bar and my camera, and head to a nearby greenspace to do some photography. It's early on a Saturday, and only one other car sits in the parking lot, the sun barely over the horizon.

I go to a bench that is next to the nature center's doors and sit. No one is there since the center won't open for a couple of hours. Perfume from the butterfly garden produces a sweet sensation in the back of my throat. The enticing aroma from wildflowers lures many bees into the garden. Birds dart in and out of feeders that hang from shepherd hooks. A gentle gurgle from the pond grants me a sense of well-being, a rare and welcome state.

I'm unaware of two eyes piercing out from under a flowery bush, eyes so huge they dwarf the face in which they are set. Then, a tiny paw reaches out, and the movement draws my attention. I watch an orange-and-white kitten emerge from the foliage and take a tentative step into the sunlight before sitting on the garden path. This small animal wants to approach but is afraid.

I sing out, "What are you doing there?"

My friendly inquiry gets answered by a mouthful of meows traveling past tiny, white teeth. Once it pegs me as trustworthy, it dashes forward and I'm thrilled until . . . until I see its left hind leg fling out in an awkward, whirligig thrust with each leap the kitten takes in my direction.

My spirit sinks. The emboldened, wee creature dashes to me if one can call the awkward forward motion a dash, and rubs its body against my hiking boot. Its constant meows beg for help, and I wonder if it knows that in its deformed kittenhood, it might not last long without a protector.

I already own a cat and can't afford the vet attention this cat needs. Besides, I am barely keeping my own life from capsizing into addiction and know I'm not in a position to help this small cat. As much as I want to help the kitten, I need to turn away. I get up and walk to my car as the cat returns to the bush.

As I sit in my vehicle deliberating over what to do, I see more cars enter the park. The kitten approaches everyone who walks near. Another woman's face lights up delightedly then turns to dismay when she sees the macabre movement from the feline. Two young people stop and want to take the cat home but argue over whether they can adopt a third pet. I can't bear to watch without helping, so I drive away. Surely someone with more resources and a bigger heart than mine will answer the kitten's call before those cries attract predators. I leave the park without having taken any photographs.

As I contemplate my decision not to help the kitten, I wonder about Mom's inability to help me. She, too, had few resources to draw upon. Maybe she wanted to help me like I wanted to help the injured feline, but didn't know how.

At home, I unlock the metal shed at the back of my single-wide mobile home and wheel a grill onto the concrete patio. I dump some charcoal onto the pan, douse it with lighter fluid, and set it aflame. The laughter of neighborhood kids as they bike on the street filters through my somber mood, and I feel less down over my inability to help the cat.

I go inside to wait for the coals to heat up and spend some time unpacking one of the remaining boxes from my move. When I open the small moving box, I find it contains a few framed photographs, one of Kurt. Today is not the day to deal with the emotions generated by seeing the smile on Kurt's face from happier times. I toss everything back in the box, shut the flaps, re-tape the lid, and move it to the back of a closet for storage.

I grab a beer, pop the top, and sit at my kitchen table. The table is at the front of my mobile home next to the bay window. Bean, sprawled on the carpeted windowsill, takes in the late-morning sun. Homes are very close to the edge of the lot in this mobile home park, and I'm only a few feet from the sidewalk and the street when I sit at the table.

I watch the kids continue their circular roam on the road. Now and then, they jump their bikes up the curb onto the sidewalk to dart past my kitchen window. I am the newcomer to their turf, and they are curious about me. I smile and wave as they pass my window.

I plate some hot dogs and head outside to begin cooking. After placing the wieners on the grill, I take a seat on the stoop to my door. Three girls stop their bikes on the sidewalk about ten feet away. The tallest one is thin with dark hair pulled back into a ponytail and looks to be about 14. One of the younger girls peers at me from under a mass of tangled locks, grins, and sticks out her tongue. I laugh.

"You live here alone?" asks the oldest.

"Who wants to know?

The girls step off their bikes and push the kickstands down.

"What'cha cooking?"

They approach, and I point to the dogs on the grill.

"I'm Lore," says the oldest. "This is my sister, Eva, and our cousin Ginny." Eva is the one with the unruly hair. She and Ginny look to be about the same age. Lore and Eva live in a trailer down the street while Ginny lives across town. Ginny's hair is neat and tied back, and her clothes are more fashionable compared to her cousins' outfits.

Eva and Ginny wander a few feet away to the tree in my yard. They bend down to poke at something on the ground.

I look at Lore and tell her, "In answer to your question, I do live here by myself."

"Why? Aren't you married?"

"Nope. I like being single."

"You got a boyfriend?"

"Not at the moment."

The two little girls return. Ginny opens her hand to show me a small worm. I also see a phone number written on her palm.

"Nice worm," I say.

Everyone's grinning. Then Eva knocks the worm off her cousin's palm and points to the phone number. "That's BJ's number. He's Ginny's boyfriend."

"Is not," Ginny says as she bats at Eva. They all start laughing. It's an infectious, no-holds-barred, full-force laugh and I find myself letting go and joining in.

They jostle each other, return to their bikes, flip up the kickstands, and yell, "Gotta go. Dinner."

The whirlwind visit from three neighborhood girls takes my mind away from the small cat I didn't help. I turn the hot dogs and think about the children's exuberant embrace of life. It makes me wonder: *If I could go into the depths of heroin use and stand close to the abyss of madness, isn't it possible for me to go just as far in the opposite direction?*

While I enjoy a cup of coffee one morning, I see a man walk by my bay window. He looks drugged but not stoned. The man lumbers sluggishly along as if he's deeply medicated. Several feet behind him dances a very charming child who can't be more than four years old. The boy delights in what he sees and makes a bold contrast to the zombielike leader of this strange, two-person pilgrimage. It's easy to focus on the lovely child and forget the apparition-like father, a man who appears to be oblivious to his surroundings and to his son. The boy sees me at my window, waves, and beams in delight when I smile and wave back.

At dusk that evening, there's a light tapping on the metal below the screen in my door. It's the child I saw walking behind his father, but his dad isn't with him. "Can I come in?" he asks.

"It's late," I tell him through the screen door. "What's your name?"

"Michael."

"Michael, I'm Valerie."

"I know. All the kids know."

"Michael, do you see anyone else outside?"

He looks around and shakes his head.

"You shouldn't be outside either. I'll walk you home."

He backs down off my stoop so I can open the door, and I step outside.

"Where do you live?"

He points down the street.

"Okay, show me."

He takes my hand, and we walk about a quarter-mile until Michael points across the street. "That's my house."

Michael's single-wide sits on a lot in need of mowing. The trailer is dark inside except for a television's flickering light. I watch Michael cross the street, open the door, and enter. When he's inside, I return home.

The next morning as I'm having breakfast in the kitchen, I see Michael's dad trudge zombielike along with Michael about three feet behind. When Michael reaches the walkway to my door, he darts away from the sidewalk, runs up the path, and calls through the screen, "Will you be my aunty?"

By the time Michael's dad realizes his son is not following him and discovers Michael at the door to my house, I have become an aunty to his four-year-old son. Later in the day, one of the girls tells me that Michael's mother, Judy, died a couple of weeks ago. Many neighbors tried to talk with Joe, Michael's father, after Judy passed, but he didn't respond. People aren't even sure Michael knows his mother will never return, and no one knows how to help them.

A couple of weeks later, I sit with Michael watching a robin's nest in the pine tree overhanging my concrete patio. Three beaks yawn out for food, and Michael is excited about seeing baby birds get fed. The parents fly away and come back with partially digested grubs, insects, and worms that they regurgitate into the open mouths.

"Aunty Val, when will the babies fly?"

"The babies need to grow flight feathers before they can leave the nest. It's called fledging when they are ready to fly." I am surprised at knowing this and at how much I'm learning about nature as I read about the natural world and go out to take pictures in the park system.

"Those baby birds eat a lot!"

"They sure do Michael, and it keeps the momma and poppa birds busy."

We see one of the parent birds across the street trying to pull a worm out of the ground. During a ferocious struggle between bird and worm, a huge shadow advances across the ground. Warning trills pour out of the trees, but it's too late. A Cooper's hawk swoops down and snatches up the bird as Michael and I watch.

Michael is horrified, screams, and begins crying. I pick him up and turn his face away from the scene. Michael sobs on my shoulder and cries out, "What's going to happen to the chicks?"

As I try to comfort him, I say, "The babies will be fine. The other parent will feed them."

My hugs and appeasing words do not work. Michael screams, "I want dad, I want dad."

My arms go numb from Michael's bellowing and squirming, but I can't put him down. His legs squeeze tight around my waist, and his arms cling harder at my neck. He won't quit sobbing or crying out for Joe. I hold him close and hurry to his father's trailer.

When I get there, I see Joe through the screen door. He's slouched on the sofa, and his eyes stare into a distance way beyond the television set in front of him. I fear that Michael's shrieks won't reach through his dad's catatonic stupor. I enter the trailer without knocking.

Michael lifts his face off my shoulder and screams at Joe about a dead momma bird. He loosens his grip on my neck, reaches one hand out in Joe's direction, and looks at his father. Tears and distress have turned Michael's face into a tight, red mass of wet and contorted features. I want so much to take his pain away from him, but I can't.

Joe's zombie head rolls up and lumbers around on his neck to face us. He looks at us without comprehension. His jaw is slack, and I fear that this situation will not end well for Michael. Then, I watch Joe's eyes travel from some hellish personal landscape to focus on Michael and his outstretched hand. Finally, the child's distress brings Joe back from wherever his mind had taken him. Joe shakes his head a few times.

Michael leans away from me toward Joe with both hands. The movement almost makes me fall, but I stumble and rebalance myself. I'm not sure what to do or say.

Just when it looks like I'll have to take Michael to his room and try to settle him down, I see Joe begin to rise off the sofa. When he's on his feet, he looks at Michael as if he's seeing him for the first time in a long time. Finally, he responds to his son's outstretched arms and wraps his own arms around Michael.

Joe kisses his son's head. "I'm sorry, I'm sorry, I'm sorry. Everything will be okay, Michael."

I see Michael's face relax, and the redness begins to subside. His howling softens into less painful sobs.

I turn, put my hand on the doorknob, look up, and see Joe's eyes reflected in the mirror hanging next to the exit. His eyes focus on me, and he mouths, "Thank you," before returning his attention to his son. Joe switches the TV off and sits down with Michael still wrapped tightly to his chest. I know Michael will be okay and that it's time for me to go.

As I walk home from Michael's trailer, I think about the mewling calls from an injured kitten and the cries from a sobbing four-year-old. I couldn't provide aid to the cat, but I helped Michael and I give the kids in my neighborhood the attention they ask of me. Maybe I'm not a bad and worthless person. Then, I consider how both the kitten and Michael reached out for help, each in their own way.

I've asked Dr. Z for help by hiring him as my therapist, and that was a good decision. He has helped me feel stronger while weakening my need for drugs. Am I strong enough to return to school? A new term approaches, and the registration deadline is close. It's time I tried going back to school, but moving has depleted my savings. I need financial help if I want to re-enroll.

Aunt Cora recently told me that Mom is doing well with them back in West Virginia. She encouraged me to try to reconnect with her. If a tiny kitten can call out for help and a four-year-old can recruit an aunty, I can reach out to Mom and ask for aid. She'll probably turn me down, but at least I need to try.

Ch. 28 - Soothing the Soul

I HAVEN'T SPOKEN TO MOM since she exploded over Dr. Z's request that she join me in a few therapy sessions. As I dial her number, I'm not hopeful that our conversation will go well.

Aunt Cora answers and puts Mom on the line. Mom asks, "How is your therapy going?"

I'm not used to my mother asking important questions about my life, and I give her a tentative response. "It's . . . uh . . . goin' okay."

"I told Cora and Pete that you're in therapy, and they think it's a good idea if you're feeling troubled. I've had to 'grin and bear' things all my life and don't understand how talking can change anything, but maybe it can."

"Mom, remember last Christmas Eve when you told me about a bible verse from Matthew?"

"Yeah?" Mom draws out her one-word response, and I know she's curious yet cautious about why I brought that up.

"Well, your minister told you about leaving the spiritually dead, and that passage from Matthew helped you leave Father to find a new life. The sermon could have been a form of counseling that helped you change your situation."

Mom is quiet for a few moments, which is an unusual response. Then, instead of her using a clichéd retort or an alienating monologue, I hear, "Valerie, you're right."

That acknowledgment means that Mom heard what I said, gave it some thought, affirmed my comment, and accepted me. I am emotionally closer to her as a result and hopeful that she'll hear my call for help.

"Mom, is this a bad time to ask a favor?" I hesitate to continue. If she won't help me, I may not be able to go back to college.

"What favor?"

"Mom, I know how important my getting an education is to you."

"Yes?" Mom seems wary.

"Mom, I'm thinking about going back to college."

At this point, I hear Mom call out to her sister and brother-in-law, "Valerie may go back to college!" She sounds happy, and I'm hopeful that she'll help me.

When her attention returns to me, she says, "Valerie, that's wonderful news."

"Mom, the thing is, I'm not sure I can afford the tuition. I have the money to buy textbooks, but I need some help with other expenses. Can you help?"

This is the moment that will decide my future, and my heart races in my chest. I expect Mom to turn me down and am stunned when I hear, "Cora and Pete talked me into putting aside some of the money from your dad's life insurance and from the sale of the house for you."

Mom's speech retreats into one of her monologues, but I'm okay with that since my mind is far away. Rather than listen, I think about how I'll be able to enroll for the fall semester. I know it will be challenging, but with Mom's financial help and Dr. Z's counseling, I might get over the fears that made me drop out.

As much as I've wanted to return to college, it's not an easy thing for me to do. I complain to Dr. Z, "I am miserable, and my insomnia is getting worse."

"How so?"

"Well, I used to wake up, lie in bed, and let my mind go blank. Now, I sort of throw myself awake and jerk up into a sitting position with the sound of my heart throbbing in my ears. I'm also breathing hard, sweating, and feeling terrified."

I think about drugs, too. But that thought doesn't get expressed to Dr. Z.

"What's waking you?"

"I'm scared about returning to school. Maybe it's too soon to go back."

"You could go part-time and take some of the pressure off yourself."

It hadn't occurred to me to tailor the experience to fit my needs. As the thought sinks in, I feel a great weight being lifted from me.

"Going to school part-time means I can keep my job in case school doesn't work out."

"You look cheerful."

I look at Dr. Z. "You know what? I'm going to enroll in only two classes, one for fun and the other to help me learn to speak in class."

"You're still looking happy. I like seeing you this way."

I shake my head and look serious as I realize something. "You know, I always thought I had to rigidly perform."

"What do you mean?"

"Well, perform in the sense of meeting others' expectations. Like my parents, . . . well, just my mom now. She assumes I'll go fulltime. Plus, taking a full load is implied in the college catalog. All the degree programs are shown in sample, fulltime semesters, but I can make up my own expectations based on my own needs."

Dr. Z looks pleased with me when he says, "That's a very sound plan, Valerie. Good work." Then, he adds, "Our time's almost up."

I begin gathering my things to leave, but Dr. Z says, "Hold on a moment. I want you to try to remember what wakes you up in a state of panic."

I register for group piano and a speech class. Then, I use some of the money Mom sent to buy a used upright piano that is no longer needed at a local elementary school. It isn't pretty, but it tunes up nicely, and the bench that comes with it contains several songbooks. One of them has traditional American folk tunes, and others feature 1960s artists like Peter, Paul and Mary.

Each evening, I play gentle, soothing melodies and go to bed hoping to sleep well. Most nights, that helps to some extent although I tend to wake earlier than I want. About a week after buying the piano, though, I jet into arousal several hours after falling asleep. I bolt upright in bed sweating and fighting to breathe. I'm terrified and sense corpselike hands reaching out from the depths of sleep to pull me back into . . . into. . .

I can't remember. Any dream images I may have had slam shut from awareness like a coffin to keep its secrets dead to me. There's some sort of nightmare at the fringes between sleep and wakefulness, something frightful, but it doesn't take shape after I wake. It leaves behind an unpleasant residue in my mind as it drifts around my subconscious and tugs to escape from its oblivious state.

When I tell Dr. Z about the nightmares that hover out of reach from my conscious awareness, he says, "Early in therapy, you mentioned an elementary-school gym teacher and custodian who lured you into the school's boiler room. Tell me more about that."

I'm puzzled by the new topic. "What does that have to do with my trouble sleeping?"

"Maybe nothing. What happened in the boiler room?"

The question triggers my heart rate, and my breathing quickens. Perspiration wets my body, a clammy chill makes me shudder, and I get an urge for a fix. "I don't remember."

It's hard to talk since I can't catch my breath. I'm shaking. I'm beginning to lose contact with the room around me. My vision becomes cloudy except for a tunnel-like circle in the center.

I choke out, "I . . . can't . . . remember." I'm scared and want to run, "Is it okay to stop talking about that?"

"It's okay, Valerie."

Dr. Z gives me time to calm down. The room comes back into focus, and I think about sailing as I center myself.

"Your insomnia is getting worse the closer you get to September and returning to school. What time of year did the gym teacher take you into the boiler room?"

"It must have been in early fall not long after school started. I remember a chilly, light rain that day. I remember the wet trees ablaze with color."

My mind opens enough for me to realize how much I dislike fall and all the colorful trees that others say they enjoy. I turn to Dr. Z and say, "I hate the fall. The trees look like an out-of-control, raging fire and they terrify me."

Ch. 29 - Hello Darkness

SEAGULLS CIRCLE THE FOUNTAIN in the pond outside the two-story, red-brick campus buildings. The modern, airy campus has replaced the aging, decrepit buildings with which it began. For several years after opening, the school held classes in structures that once housed a veterans' hospital. Today, students rather than injured soldiers linger in the September sunshine and reunite with classmates they haven't seen since spring. My return to the place from which I bolted in terror slams me into a fissure between flight and fight. I need to find a way to stay. I need to find a way to fight.

Near the theater entrance, I go left and head to the liberal arts wing. Inside the building, atrium windows pour sunshine into the common area and create a bright, hopeful atmosphere. The collective excitement of returning students sends positive energy throughout the cavernous room and makes me realize how much I've missed being on campus.

The enjoyment of my first day back in school dissolves when I get near the battleground classroom where I will confront my fear of speaking. Entering the room is like going into the Roman colosseum and invokes internal, predatory lions that will, most likely, find me easy prey. Adrenaline signals flight, but I find a seat and await my fate.

On the first day of most classes, students aren't asked to do much, and that's what I'm hoping for as the professor enters. He hands out a syllabus and goes over the course requirements. When he asks us to introduce ourselves by stating our names and why we're taking the class, I slouch way down into my seat feeling defeated already.

The carnage approaches row-by-row, seat-by-seat, name-by-name, comment-by-comment, until getting slain would be preferable to speaking my name. I'm doomed to talk next and wipe my sweaty palms on my jeans, look down at my desk, and mumble, "I'm Valerie."

My voice shakes. "I'm here because . . ." I take a deep breath, "because I'm terrified, . . . which scares me." *Huh? That doesn't even make sense.* My brow tightens, and my eyes moisten. I'm ready to berate my stupid incompetence but remember Dr. Z's advice to tell myself positive statements. *I'm doing my best. I'm not running away from this class (yet); and I can, at least, be proud of that.*

My lips tighten and my chin comes up as I try to stay focused. When the last person in class finishes her introduction, the instructor talks about how hard public speaking is for many people. He asks us to take out a sheet of paper and write about any fears we have about the course.

Most students jot something down, gather up their things, and dash off, but several students remain. I'm not the only one who needs more time to let the instructor know about their speech anxiety.

Dr. Z congratulates me on speaking in class, but I'm not proud of my initial speech performance. I'm hurt and petulant. "This is too damn hard."

"What is?"

"Fighting my fears. And, I don't see my horrible speech as an accomplishment."

"Why not?"

Anger takes over. "My voice shook when I spoke in class, and my comment didn't make sense. I looked and felt like a total idiot."

"So what if your voice shook?"

"I was embarrassed and scared. I hate myself for looking foolish."

Dr. Z, who rarely lectures, says, "You did your best even if your best wasn't as good as many of the other students. No one, certainly not you, needs to be ashamed over doing their best. On top of it, you faced your fears and have a lot to be proud of."

"Okay." It's a concession I need to make if I want to embrace a more positive attitude, one that will help me return to that speech arena. "I didn't leave class although I wanted to. And . . . and . . . I did speak!" My chin tilts up, and my fist hits the chair's arm to punctuate my comments. "Yeah, and damn it – I did do my best even if my best doesn't measure up to the other students' performances!"

I'm beaming when I tell Dr. Z, "I tested out of the beginning piano course and got placed into the next level up."

Then, everything changes and my outgoing happiness retracts into a silent anxiousness.

"What are you thinking, Valerie?"

"I love the piano class but am scared about the solo we need to do for our final."

"That's months away. Take it one day at a time," Dr. Z advises.

He chuckles, and I look up. "If there was a prize for worrying, you would get it, Valerie"

He's right. As angry as my situation makes me, I need to take one day at a time instead of worrying about something scheduled to occur several months from now.

When I show up for my second speech class, a sign on the closed door indicates the class will meet in room 107 further down the hallway. The new room contains round tables rather than rows of desks. The teacher greets us and instructs, "For a few weeks, we'll work on brief, timed, informal speeches in small groups. Brief means up to three minutes. A timer will use a stopwatch to signal the speaker when time is up. At three minutes, you're to wind down if you haven't already finished. Informal means you'll stay seated in your group rather than stand behind a lectern."

The steps for an informal speech seem manageable, and I'm encouraged by that.

"I'm assigning people to groups of six. As I read your name, gather with your group, and then find a table."

When I hear my name and find my group, I notice it's made up of the students who remained longer at the end of the first class. We are the ones who wrote more about our speech anxieties. We find a table and take a seat. The instructor passes out stopwatches, one for each table. "Today, begin by getting acquainted with the members of your group and using the stopwatch. Everyone needs to know how to time speeches." For about ten minutes, the room fills with voices as we talk in small groups and pass the stopwatch around.

"All right, folks, quiet down." The instructor waits for the student chatter to stop. A couple of classmates shush particularly boisterous groups.

When the teacher regains our attention, he tells us, "Take fifteen minutes to write out an outline for your first mini-speech. Pick a sport or hobby you enjoy and explain what it is you like about it. There's enough time so that everyone should be able to do this today."

I jot down a few lines of speech, but more important is adding a strategy to the written outline. I draw a rainbow, some smiley faces with thumbs up, and a few notes of encouragement like "Way to go," "You can do this," and "Hang in there," on the notes for my mini-speech,

When the others in my group begin their speeches, I take deep breaths to settle my body's flight response and distract myself by squeezing a small stone. Both techniques, suggested by Dr. Z, help me concentrate on what the other students talk about.

When it's my turn to speak, I look down and away from everyone for a moment before managing to say, "I enjoy photography." I'm immediately out of breath and look at my drawing of a smiling face and take another deep breath. "I see more when I take photos." The students at my table are patient and empathize with my difficulty. When I look up, a couple of them look away to give me space as I flounder, but others put their thumbs up, nod approval, and appear to be urging me on.

I remind myself that what I have to say is important, and continue, "Light is the key to photography, and light is also key to understanding the world. Thank you."

The timer announces, "88 seconds." My mini-speech wasn't great, had long pauses, and didn't make much sense, but it's a start. The others in my group applaud politely while a couple of students add some back-slapping and high fives that make me smile. We bond as we help each other get over whatever fears we brought to speaking in class.

I search through the music I have on hand for a tune to play during my piano finals. One of the songbooks contains some music Uncle Pete played one afternoon when I helped him in his wood-working shop several years ago. A single piece of music stands out because Uncle Pete got so caught up when he heard it that he stopped working and pretended to be a symphony conductor. Later, Uncle Pete told me that Paul Simon wrote the lyrics to the song when he was only 21. The memory is a good one, and I look over the score for "The Sound of Silence." It looks doable yet challenging enough to fulfill the course requirements.

The opening lyrics seem depressing, but when I begin unpacking the song note-by-note, measure-by-measure, I discover a rich, emotional layering that creates hope. After getting a general feel for the tune, I concentrate on the single bass and treble notes underpinning the first verse. The lyrics play out in the bass area with a tentative, almost timid accompaniment in the treble range. Bass and treble combine to form a duet played two notes at a time, one from each hand, that goes on until the second verse. That first verse is lovely and gentle, and I practice it before going to bed. I'm hopeful that the music will soothe my soul enough that I can fall asleep fast and stay asleep.

I'm in extreme danger, and the shadowy form pursuing me will destroy me if I'm caught. I have never been so frightened, and my life depends on outrunning the terrible man who chases me. I run across a field edged by trees ablaze with fiery-colored leaves and look for somewhere to hide. A log cabin materializes, and I sprint inside where I curl up in a nook behind the fireplace. I wrap my arms around my knees to make myself small, and I try to quiet my heavy breathing. Maybe I won't be found if I'm still and silent.

There's a tiny chink between the logs behind me, and I look through it to see if the man is still coming. He is. When I entered the cabin, I thought it was safe and secure, but it's not. The logs making up the cabin walls shift and grow apart. The man sees me. I scrunch down as tiny as I can make myself, but I know I'm doomed. The man's huge face, its features obscured in shadow, appears close to where I'm hiding. The man carries a weapon, a baseball bat, and he lifts it ready to. . .

I bolt awake. My heart races, my breathing is quick, and I'm sweating, but at least I now know why I wake terrified.

Dr. Z listens to me recount the cabin nightmare. Then, I give him the details of a second dream that occurred the night following the first one.

"I'm in an upstairs bedroom at my parents' house on a chilly, autumn day. Rain slashes at the windows and pounds on the roof. I get out of bed to ensure the windows are shut tight and see water pouring down the walls. There are holes everywhere in the ceiling, and icy rainwater gushes into the room. The roof needs to be repaired but the damage increases so fast that I soon see through the roof rafters. Someone yells at me for creating the mess and begins coming after me. I hide in a closet filled with buckets and mops, hoping I won't be found, but I hear sloshing as the angry man approaches. When the closet doorknob turns, I'm too scared to stay asleep and wake up horrified."

"How old are you in the dreams?"

"I'm young, just a child."

I begin to wonder whether my dream represents my elementary-school trauma. Dr. Z doesn't say anything, and I'm grateful for the space he gives me to process things that have been buried for so long inside my mind.

I ask, "Is it possible that the fiery trees, fireplace, mops, and buckets represent the boiler room where I faced the school's custodian and gym teacher?"

How could it be possible since I don't remember what happened in that boiler room so long ago?

"That seems possible, Valerie."

Dr. Z adds, "Being attacked in a dream often symbolizes feeling vulnerable and insecure."

"Why was one nightmare set in my parents' house?"

Dr. Z waits for me to think about an answer to my question. "Geez, it represents the damage Dad did to me, doesn't it?"

I hate having to deal with this. "Damn it," I say, "this stuff is messing with my sleep and making my days difficult. And, I still feel scared, vulnerable, and powerless. I don't need friggin' reminders about it in my sleep."

When I look at Dr. Z, he indicates, "You're no longer a scared child. You're an adult with many skills. There are other ways for the nightmares and your life to play out."

Ch. 30 - Restless Dreams

"MUSIC IS A NONVERBAL METHOD of expressing thoughts and emotions," says my piano instructor during her lecture. "Music can soothe the soul. Research," she says, "indicates that listening to or playing music decreases blood pressure and heart rate. It can lessen anxiety and stress, too. Strong, dissonant music acts as a pressure valve to release pent up anger. Music therapists find that music helps those with PTSD by rewiring the body's neural networks along beneficial pathways. Music can motivate, as in the military or on the football field, or help with movement in physical therapy. Can anyone give an example from their own life of music as a motivator or as an aid to movement?"

While other students raise their hands and provide answers, I think about one of the times when Michael stayed overnight and dawdled in the morning instead of getting ready to meet his dad. I played some lively music and asked him to brush his teeth and change from his pajamas to the beat of the music. He took up the challenge, quit messing around, and got ready to meet his father on time.

"Good examples," says the professor to the students who spoke up. I sigh and wish I had had the courage to tell the class about Michael.

"Music is widespread and has a lengthy history," continues the professor. "In fact, human beings may bond with the beat of music from the moment the fetus hears the mother's heartbeat in the womb."

Her lecture makes sense, and many students add comments about how music impacts them or someone they know.

That evening, as I practice "The Sound of Silence" for my final, I discover an intriguing change in the musical score. I concentrate on the second verse and marvel at how the musical notation switches from lyrics played in the bass area to lyrics played in the treble range. At that point, the song's main theme goes from being played by the left hand to play by the right hand. The second verse also goes from the gentle, single notes of the first verse to bold, confident chords that resonate from the piano. My body leans forward while playing as if I'm trying to embrace the emotions that go along with the words and music. The powerful emotions I experience exhaust me, and I'm hopeful of getting more than a few hours' sleep.

It's a lovely day in early autumn. The trees haven't yet turned color, and the day retains the warmth of summer. Meadow grasses are tall, and I'm biking down a country lane to a nearby forest.

When I arrive at the woods, I lean my bike against the trunk of a large oak tree and sit next to some willow saplings on the bank of a gently moving brook. I take off my shoes and socks and push my toes into the cool, pebbly sand.

Someone approaches, but I do not panic because he is someone I recognize. The man sits next to me and smiles, but the smile isn't right. His eyes harbor an intent that backs up into his face and turns his attempt at a grin into a terrifying rictus.

I try to get up and move away, but he grabs me and asks, "What's your hurry?" He forces me to sit on his lap and begins squirming and breathing hard. He moves his hand across my waist and slips it into my waistband. Just when I'm ready to project my mind outward and mentally sink below the surface of the stream to escape the unwanted attention, a police officer appears. She draws her gun and orders the man to let me go, but he doesn't. Instead, he brandishes a knife and threatens to slice my throat.

I scream, "Kill him! Kill him!"

The officer takes careful aim as the man sneers, "You'll miss me and hit her instead." She pulls the trigger on her service revolver, the bullet whizzes past my ear, and the man behind me jerks as his grip on me falters. I am free from the horrible man who wanted to hurt me and elated by the officer's actions. I even do the Rocky Balboa dance on the shore of the brook as I celebrate the man's death.

The intensity of my gleeful "kill" emotions jolts me awake. I sit up sweating, panting, and feeling dread over my reaction to a man's death.

At my next therapy session, I tell Dr. Z, "The part of the nightmare where I scream, 'Kill him!' 'Kill him!' scares me."

"Why?"

"I should feel evil for being happy about the predatory man getting executed, but I don't feel bad about it in the dream."

"It's a dream, Valerie. Police officers are trained to kill when their or someone else's life is in danger. Your life was in danger during the nightmare."

Dr. Z is right.

"What other interpretations do you see in the dream?"

It's a great question. "Well, . . . I can see two possibilities. The 'kill' theme represents destroying a dark part of myself that's been deeply troubling and hard to change."

"Good," says Dr. Z. "You're saying that symbolically, the dream means you're killing the illness you carry inside. What about the second interpretation you thought of?"

"The dream could represent a form of justice. As much as I wish a police officer could have brought those who hurt me to justice, I know that's not possible. Dad is dead, and I don't know the names of the gym teacher and custodian who hurt me. Besides, that was fifteen or more years ago."

"Anything else?"

"I guess the dream means I no longer blame myself but know I got hurt by others. What happened to me wasn't my fault."

"Did other emotions occur in your dream?"

It wasn't until Dr. Z asked that question that I acknowledge how much anger was behind my yelling for the officer to kill the man holding a knife at my throat. "Dr. Z, it opened up a lot of angry feelings, feelings I'm not sure I know what to do with."

Attending speech and piano classes makes me balance a desire to run from the finals that will put me in public view with managing my fears. On top of that dilemma or under it or fueling it are angry impulses. I decide to work them off in the privacy of the racquetball court. I rent the equipment at the college gymnasium, enter the court alone, close the door, and smash away at the ball. The fast movement and the smacking sound of the ball against the racquet and the wall help channel the anger in ways that do not harm me or anyone else. I leave the court sapped of energy but ready to focus on my upcoming finals.

Over the semester, I've given longer speeches within my group of speech-anxious students who have become comrades in arms. We encourage and celebrate our successes and have moved on to doing short speeches at the lectern in front of the entire class.

In piano class, I've been called on occasionally to play a solo piece of music, which helps prepare me for my final. I supplement those successes with practice at home. My fingers seem to know the notes I'm learning for my final, so I don't constantly read the score in front of me. A neural memory has formed which I hope will fire off and assist me during my final, solo performance. I still practice each night before going to bed.

I'm driving, listening to music, and looking forward to seeing my relatives in West Virginia. About 90 miles away from the Ohio River, the road enters hills and makes many sharp curves as it hugs the steep hillside. I slow down to a speed under the posted limit because I'm unfamiliar with the twists and turns I'm encountering.

In my rearview mirror, I see a fiery red truck come up behind me to tailgate my bumper. There's no way for the driver to pass since the curves keep anyone from seeing oncoming traffic. Then, the tailgating driver begins honking and hitting the rear of my car with his truck. I pull off the road at the next scenic overlook, but the truck doesn't keep going. Instead, it blocks my car from getting back on the road.

I lock the doors and close the windows, but the man gets out with a hammer and knocks out the glass on the passenger side of my vehicle. There's enough room on my side between his truck and my car to crack open the door and squeeze out.

I don't run. I face the man as he comes at me. His mouth snarls and appears more animal-like than human. As he approaches, he unbuckles his belt and unzips his pants. The stench from his crotch provides a clear and close sign of predatory danger.

He removes his belt and forms a noose with it. He isn't expecting me to fight and doesn't see my bayonet until I raise it ready to stab. I watch as fear crosses his face, and then I knife him over and over and over until . . .

The mixture of intense hatred and fear of what I'm doing breaks me free from the nightmare. My eyes fly open, and I'm awake. Although the dream changed from fear of being harmed to bravely protecting myself, my physical reaction is the same. I'm panting for breath, sweating, and feeling my heart beat wildly in my chest.

As I tell Dr. Z about this nightmare, I am upbeat and celebratory. Then, it hits me that my gleeful reaction to killing someone, even if it's in a dream, isn't right.

"Is it wrong to be happy about killing my perpetrator?"

Dr. Z says, "They are dreams. You aren't actually murdering anyone."

"Yes, of course, but it feels very wrong."

"Valerie, I'm not an attorney, but from what I understand, killing someone when your life is in danger is legal and justified."

"It is true that I'm defending myself in the dream and . . ." I pause as it sinks into my conscious being that ". . . my defense is justifiable."

"Definitely," says Dr. Z. "Keep in mind that committing violence in a dream expresses anger."

"I am angry over what happened to me, and I have a right to be," I say as my fist hits the arm of the chair.

"The nightmare could also be anger over unfulfilled goals, especially if there are unjust roadblocks to those goals."

Dr. Z pauses and gives me time to think about what he said.

"Geez, I could be very angry over how difficult it is for me to confront my fears so that I can get a college degree."

Dr. Z advises, "Valerie, you've taken control of your fears in your dreams. Maybe it symbolizes that you're taking back control of your life."

I know that the awful things done to me as a child will always be a part of who I am. I can either remain justifiably stunted and angry about what can never change in my past, or I can take control. Something snakes around inside my head squirming for recognition. Trauma destroyed my ability to trust others, and it severed me from normal social relations for a long time. It destroyed my self-confidence and made me hate myself to the point where I tried to self-destruct with drugs. All those losses clamor for recognition.

I hurry home burdened by what I lost and wanting to grieve those losses in private. Loud and angry sobs heave up from and cough out of a place deep inside of me. I double up and hug my knees as I sit in the hallway of my mobile home, back to the wall. Agonizing sobs express remorse for a lost childhood and an adulthood I almost threw away when I used drugs. Family violence and the trauma I experienced at school stole so much from me, but I am ready to take back my life and reclaim what was stolen.

Ch. 31 - Finals

TOO MUCH DEAD TIME at work leaves my mind unoccupied, so I fill the vacant hours with images from recent, vivid nightmares. Those unnerving dreams carry my thoughts so far away that it takes a while to register the noise in my office. At first all I hear is a dull, distant sound, but the sound keeps repeating and eventually gets my attention. I snatch up the phone. "Mr. Jenson's office. Valerie speaking."

"Hello, Valerie."

Kurt's voice rushes past the defenses I had erected to keep from thinking about him. My mind goes from thinking about nightmares to remembering the sensual pleasure of Kurt's warm breath on my ear, his tentative touch pushing my hair from my cheek, his soft lips on mine, and his skin next to mine.

I take several shallow, quick breaths of air. *I should hang up without speaking to him.*

"Valerie, are you there?"

"Hi, Kurt."

"I want to see you."

I want to see him. I want what we once shared before drugs became problematic.

I hear people talking in the background at Kurt's end but their voices are garbled by traffic noise. Kurt's mouth, so close to the telephone, conveys a nervous, raspy breath that bears a slight wheeze. The street sounds in the background suggest a rootlessness and the wheezing indicates ill health, and both sounds remind me of Kurt's situation. I know from Skipper that Kurt hasn't contacted him for help with treatment.

I can't see Kurt. I can't do that to myself. Or can I? Maybe he will quit if . . . if what?

"Valerie?"

As much as I'd like to join Kurt again to look for the sun's fire as it pierces through icicles or feel the sexual energy of sitting next to him at the piano or capture frost on early morning photo shoots, I know I can't because I'd probably use his drugs again, too.

"Valerie?" Kurt's voice rises a few notches, and I hear a hint of desperation.

It's not a good idea to talk with him, but I do. "Are you in treatment?"

I listen to the slight rumbling coming from Kurt's chest as he breathes. The wheeze is audible even through the background noises. Finally, Kurt says, "If we get back together, I'll get treatment. Okay? John and Alice said you moved, but they don't know where you are. Please let me visit."

I calm my breathing, center myself, and squeeze a plastic bottle on my desk to redirect my weakening will into some form of strength. I know that letting Kurt back into my life would make me susceptible to another overdose, to skipping work or school for drugs, and to facing the abyss where the horror of using a needle felt grim-reaper close.

"Valerie, I'm only using occasionally now and know I can quit if you'll help me."

If I try to reason with him by reminding him that Skipper will help him, we will enter a bizarre merry-go-round exchange during which I might give in to Kurt. It's better to stay free of such a sticky web of conversation.

"I can't help you, Kurt. I'm having difficulty helping myself. I need to go."

"VALERIE," he shouts as he tries to keep me on the phone.

It hurts, but I put the receiver down. I sit at my desk free from Kurt's phone call but not free from the pain. I push my chair back and double over gasping for breath.

After several minutes, I reach for my squeeze bottle to refocus my attention to something concrete in the room. I sit up, get my school notebook, and work on my final speech. It's not easy to concentrate, but I push out one word and only one word at a time. What appears on paper isn't a speech but punched out phrases of pain that ultimately turn into words of anger. I rip up the paper, decide to take a break, and head outdoors. As I pass through the revolving doors at the base of the building, I look for the veteran who received my secret Santa gift about a year ago. I haven't seen him for months. The ache I feel for Kurt and for this veteran stirs such fury onto my face that no one, not even a panhandler, approaches me as I try to walk off the agony I feel.

Piano finals are one week away, and I find enough courage to raise an issue with the instructor during class. "I hear that performers often deal with nerves before going on stage, and I'm anxious about our final. Any advice on how to deal with performance anxiety?"

"Well," says the piano teacher, "you can try taking an aspirin or two a few hours before your class solo." The advice is unsatisfactory, but I let it go. I'm not happy about being advised to use pills even if they are over-the-counter ones found in almost every bathroom medicine cabinet.

The student at the piano next to me says, "I need something stronger than a couple of aspirins to get through my final," and he mimics downing a drink. His comment and gesture get an outburst of laughter from the class. Later, that student taps me on the shoulder as we leave the classroom.

"Good question, . . . the one you asked in class," he says as he motions me to one side of the hallway. He moves close to me and whispers, "I've got some mild downers. They can help if you're nervous."

As nervous as I am about finals, I find his offer hard to pass up. After all, I don't have to use the pills. "Okay, lay 'em on me."

He pulls a prescription bottle from his backpack, dumps out a few pills, and hands them over. I stuff them into one of my pockets.

He tells me his name is Bill and asks, "Wanna grab a coffee?"

"Uh, yeah, coffee sounds good, but I can't stay long."

I find a table in the cafeteria and watch Bill grab two cups of coffee. He jokes with the staff behind the cash register and nods to other students as he passes them. He's pleasant and engaging but he is also someone who offers pills to strangers.

After Bill sets our coffees down, he takes a seat and stirs some sugar into his java. He asks, "What are you playing for your piano final?"

"A Paul Simon tune."

"Who's Paul Simon?"

"He was part of Simon and Garfinkle."

"Oh, I've heard of them."

It doesn't take long to discover that Bill knows little about 1960s folk music, so that conversational topic dies fast.

"Bill, what are you playing for the final?"

"Honestly, I haven't decided."

"Wow, you must play pretty well if you're leaving that decision go."

"Not really, but I'll figure something out."

Bill sounds like someone who doesn't care about his education, so I begin putting on my coat. "Valerie, before you go, can I have your phone number?"

"How 'bout you write yours down so I don't have to dig out some paper."

He scribbles out his name and phone number on a napkin and hands it over. I fold it and tuck the napkin into the pocket where I shoved the pills. "Thanks for the coffee. I need to go work on something for speech class, so I'll see you during finals week."

When I get home, I put the pills and Bill's phone number into an envelope before shoving them into my medicine cabinet. I don't have to take the pills, but I can keep them as a backup plan if finals go badly.

I've decided to talk about my family and had outlined a few preliminary ideas on note cards. It's time I flesh out my speech final.

Spider-Web Nirvana

Final Assignment – Speech 101

Hello, I'm Valerie Willis, and I often wonder how my West Virginia family found itself outside the American Dream even as that dream wove its dictates straight-jacket tight around us. Instead of experiencing affluence and upward mobility, we became numbed out by need, pain, and shame. As a result, we felt hurt and abandoned by our culture. The harm we felt made us hurt each other and ourselves. We drank, and we did drugs. We

> didn't like each other much as if it was our fault that we didn't rise easily to reach the American Dream.

I could go on to describe how we hurt each other and abused alcohol and drugs, but that speech about my family is one that nobody wants to hear. In addition, it probably won't earn a good grade, so I rethink it.

As I think about my final, I decide to wear Mom's class ring while giving the speech. It symbolizes Mom's high regard for education, and I want to honor her desire for me to get a college degree. I also wear the ring to help center myself when I get nervous during my speech. I've practiced fingering and squeezing it in order to bring me out of and away from the anxiety going on in my head. At such times, it forms a physical anchor that reconnects me to the external, concrete world and the task I'm doing.

Squeezing the hardness of Mom's ring also reminds me how she was made hard and self-contained by the harms in her life. It's a different type of hard edge from Dad's, and it expressed itself in unimaginative, uninspired behavior that stuck closely to the dictates required by her roles as wife and mother. She cooked basic meat-and-potato meals, she fed me at the appropriate times, she cleaned on a rigid schedule, she clothed me in plain yet functional styles, and she packed dad's lunch pail every day. Her hard edge made her retreat to "fortune-cookie proverbs" such as "if the milk's free, why buy the cow," a phrase she used when I became sexually active.

I decide to talk about the hardness in my life with a focus on Dad.

I'm prepared when the instructor introduces me. I gather my notecards, go to the lectern, and hear him announce the title of my speech.

<u>Strength Forged in Fire</u>

> Hello, I'm Valerie Willis, and this is my dad's bayonet from the Vietnam conflict.

I pull the knife from its sheath and display it to the class. One trick I use at the lectern is to provide a visual that directs audience attention away from me to whatever I'm displaying. My classmates look at the knife instead of at me, which lessens my anxiety and allows me to feel less vulnerable while I'm in front of them. I take a breath and look at my notes.

> When I inherited this knife, the horrors of the Vietnam combat flashed into my mind. My father survived that war but brought home invisible scars. His sense of survivor's guilt tormented him throughout his life, and that torment often spilled out angrily onto me and my mother. When my father died and I inherited his bayonet, I didn't want it and hid it in the back of my closet. My aunt, though, helped me recognize that knives have many uses and meanings and that someday I might discover a deeper understanding of my dad and his combat knife.

I pause to do some deep breathing, calm myself, and create space for my audience to wonder what I may have discovered. I touch Mom's class ring for a second or two before turning to the next note card and continuing my speech.

> Bayonets, of course, are used to kill, to sever people from their lives. I know this knife functioned in that capacity during the Vietnam conflict. Knives, in a different sense, cut away excess material as when trimming fat from a steak. They can pierce to the center of things, like a cantaloupe, or symbolize cutting through to the truth underneath layers of uncertainties. They can butter bread, and they can skin a deer.

There's a short pause as I turn to the next note card. On that card, I wrote a note to myself:

Keep going. This is important and interesting.

A slight smile forms on my face, a subtle gesture more to myself than to my audience, and I continue.

> Dad's bayonet, of course, reminds me of him. He was an unhappy man who made me fear him.

I brandish the knife a bit which draws a few nervous gasps from the audience, and then I place it back in its sheath. I enjoy the little drama that engaged the audience with what I'm saying.

> Yeah, Dad made life tough for me and my mom, but he did something else in the process. Just like this bayonet's strength came from being forged in fire, I inherited a strength forged in Dad's fiery temperament.

My voice shakes a little because of the personal revelation, so I take a brief pause and look at my writing on the last note card for my speech. It encourages:

Keep going. This is important to say, and it's interesting.

> That strength doesn't always make me feel sharp. In fact, I'm often down and dull instead, but I know that I have an inner fortitude to unsheathe when necessary. I can't always gather that power on my own. Sometimes I need the help of relatives, friends, and neighbors to draw out my strength, and sometimes I lean on the help of a therapist. All in all, Dad's bayonet symbolizes my fiery connection to him as well as to other, more nurturing, relationships. Drawing on my tough inheritance keeps me forging ahead whenever I want to give up. Thank you.

My fellow students applaud enthusiastically, and it's clear they liked my speech. Maybe they even liked me a little, too.

I am in my piano class waiting to do my solo, and anticipatory anxiety takes precedence over relaxing. I have practiced "The Sound of Silence" to the point where my mind often becomes divorced from the music on the page as my fingers find their way through the piano's keys without my willing them to do so. Still, it's maddening to keep my nerves in check as I wait my turn. I squeeze Mom's ring to help me concentrate on the other students who are performing before me. My solo is scheduled to occur about halfway through the program. As I listen, I keep bouncing between feeling confident about my upcoming solo and fearing that I'll freeze up rather than play.

The first student performance is technically correct, note for note, but lacks emotional depth. The students who follow that initial solo sometimes make mistakes but keep going. Two students stop momentarily after playing a wrong note before they continue. It's good to see how others handle their mistakes. Their unintended role modeling means I can stop and regroup if necessary, as they did. I do not need to be perfect. I only need to do my best and get through this.

When I'm called upon to perform, I sit quietly at the piano for a few moments to center myself. I love the music I've been preparing, and I actually want to play this piece, music that means so much to me. This tune made me aware of the nightmares undergirding my insomnia, and it helped me gain insights into what haunts my mind.

I take a quick look at Mom's ring on my finger before leaning forward to play. I turn my head slightly to hear the gentle, slow-moving notes that open the piece. When the transition occurs from those soft beginning tones to bold musical chords, I straighten up and unpack the interplay of light and dark notes and the melodic unfolding of expressive major chords. My spirit soon intertwines with each chord and note released by my fingers, and I close my eyes to enjoy the flight through the piano piece. When I finish, I'm happy about my musical translation of the tune, the one that freed me from the tyranny of buried nightmares. My eyes meet Bill's, and I know that we are not destined to get together. I bet he knows that, too. His performance had lacked commitment or depth.

When the last soloist finishes playing, the teacher thanks us for our efforts, hands out comments on our performances, and wishes us a wonderful break. The instructor had written excellent on my comment sheet and asked me to stop by her office.

After saying goodbye to my classmates, I go next door to see the piano professor. Her office has floor-to-ceiling bookcases on one wall and a desk opposite the books. Two overstuffed chairs for visitors sit next to a window. Light, fluffy snowflakes float through the cold air outside. I tap on the open door, and she looks up. She motions me in, and I take a seat while she finishes an email. When she turns to me, she remarks, "You performed very well and should be taking private lessons."

Her comment about my playing pleases me even though I can't afford private lessons, which is something I do not tell her. Still, it's wonderful to know that I have some musical abilities.

She asks, "What are your career plans?"

"I'm not yet sure. I just returned to school and need to figure that out."

"If you ever consider a career in music, I'd be happy to discuss various options with you any time you'd like."

"Thanks, I'll keep that in mind."

It's a pleasant office and now that the semester is over, there's time to relax. I ask about the photos of children displayed on her bookcase, and she tells me the two girls in the photographs are her kids, ages five and seven. I tell her a little about the kids in my neighborhood, and about Mom, Aunt Cora, and Uncle Pete. I don't tell her anything about the darker aspects of my life.

Our conversation is light and friendly. She tells me how she chose being a music teacher as her career, and I realize how much easier her life has been compared to mine. It's clear that she didn't need to fight to overcome any hardship in order to pursue her dreams. She takes for granted that a young person naturally gets a college education and chooses a career. It's obvious she envisions higher education in her own children's futures.

Suddenly, I despise her for the apparent ease with which she had access to privileges and benefits that others, like myself, do not. I begin to wonder if Mom and Dad hadn't been so hard pressed to survive economically, that they may have been kinder, more nurturing parents. It's not fair that some people, like her and her children, have it easy. She doesn't even seem aware of the hardship that stands in the way of some and makes life more difficult for them.

The irritation I feel wants immediate expression. Blowing up at her would, obviously, put her off, remove her as an ally, and ultimately hurt me rather than her. I have to stuff the destructive impulse and desire for a furious outburst. I realize that I can't create a better life for myself if I express my resentment. It's better that I leave her office rather than chance expressing any negativity, so I look at my watch and point out, "Oh, I'm late for an appointment. I'm sorry, but I need to go."

"Valerie, thank you for stopping by. Have a wonderful holiday break."

Although I prefer venting my displeasure more fully, all I say in return is goodbye. I do not thank her for her encouragement or wish her a good holiday break. I leave her office and find a quiet spot to sit awhile. I think back to how awkward I initially felt in Kurt's environment as if the upscale surroundings in his Dad's condo would reject me. If it hadn't been for getting familiar and comfortable with the trappings of the middle class during my time with Kurt, I wondered if I would have successfully navigated my way back to college and countered the impulses to hurt the piano teacher who only wanted to help me.

Once I back away from my anger at my music teacher, I'm able to enjoy my successful return to school. The completion of my coursework produces a high that I suspect will last much longer than any drug high. On the way to my vehicle, I catch a glimpse of myself reflected in the windows outside the campus theater, and I like the person I see mirrored there.

Ch. 32 - The Edge of Capsize

I COMBINE A FEW vacation days with the Christmas holiday break from work to visit Mom, Aunt Cora, and Uncle Pete in West Virginia. My Aunt's kitchen, the center of her home, is often filled with the scent of baking bread. This time, the fragrances of cinnamon, nutmeg, and ginger waft around as I help Aunt Cora make pumpkin pies and gingerbread cookies. Mom sits at the kitchen table drinking tea and watching my aunt and me as we bake and prepare the traditional turkey meal. When my aunt and I talk about our lives and current events, Mom finds it difficult to join in. Whenever she tries, we go silent until she's through with her monologue way of speaking. Aunt Cora gets in an occasional question in an attempt to introduce a two-way dialogue, but it doesn't work.

I know Mom is happy living with her sister and doing some bookkeeping for Uncle Pete, but she cannot step far outside the cocoon she had to wrap protectively around her. My gratitude for her financial help makes me pat her hand and give her hugs in an attempt to reach her, but they are hugs and touches she doesn't know how to return. Physical closeness seems to fluster her, but I understand.

Mom has had to protect herself so fiercely and for so long that she cannot emerge from the protective threads that bind her to herself, but I'm pleased to see how often she looks at her high school ring on my finger. Aunt Cora tells me that my wearing that ring gives Mom a great deal of satisfaction.

I return to Cleveland feeling hopeful about the new year until my boss calls me into his office several days before my classes are to begin. He tells me he will retire at the end of June but assures me that the company will find a place for me. Unfortunately, the two afternoons I take off each week to see Dr. Z and attend school will have to stop after he retires, because I will need to work fulltime if I wish to stay with my employer.

My employer has been generous during my therapy with Dr. Z, and I'm grateful for that, but I am unmoored by the impending change. I rely on regular counseling to keep from backsliding into my fears or my need to self-medicate with street drugs. If I quit working rather than stay on fulltime, I'll lose the benefits that help pay for counseling. If I quit to go to school, I'll head into uncharted areas with no guarantee I'll find a major or even finish a degree. Facing an unknown future if I leave my job scares the hell out of me.

My dark side, the part of me that I worked so hard to put at a distance, returns. The feeling of being haunted from within sends me into a tailspin, and I drag myself around through each long second of each long minute of the day. As I worry about what to do about work, I begin feeling the sensation of a needle entering my arm. The pull toward drugs makes me think about visiting my old apartment building where I'm sure Mitch and Janet are still dealing in narcotics. Too frequently, I open my medicine cabinet and pull out the envelope of pills that Bill, the student in my piano class, gave me last semester. His phone number is on the envelope, and I bet that means I could get more pills from him if I want them. So far, I've avoided driving to Mitch and Janet's and am able to leave the pills Bill gave me untouched. I do drink more often and more heavily than I have in months.

I drink too much and am hung over when the new semester begins. At least I do not stagger when I enter the ice-glazed doors to the science wing, stamp snow off my boots, and spend a moment in the warmth from the heaters immediately inside the doors before heading to class. I've eased up this semester by taking courses that do not require presentations or performances. Now, rather than demanding finals, my uncertain future sends pulses of anxiety through me as I lumber down the campus corridor.

On my way to astronomy, a class that fulfills my science requirement, I stop by the cafeteria to top off my travel mug with black coffee. I need caffeine to help eliminate the alcohol-induced fog in my brain. The aroma of fresh, hot java perks me up as I leave the cafeteria and pass an information board so covered in old flyers that I take comfort in how it mirrors the havoc in my mind. Out of the chaos on that board, though, something stands out that taps into a pleasant memory of Kurt and his father. I stop and take a couple of steps back to look for whatever caught my attention. Peeking out from layers of announcements for events that occurred last semester, I see a stylized drawing of a sailboat, and it calls to me like a siren to a sailor.

I slide out of my back pack, place it on the floor, crack open my coffee mug, and take a sip as I go through the mayhem of flyers. When I salvage the submerged sailboat flyer from the sea of papers, I read:

Learn to Sail
College Sailing Club
Boat School Lectures:
Wed. @ 6:00, Room 211, Science Building
Fall Sailing School
Sat. @ 1:00, Lake Baseline
Contact Kevin @ 555-5555

The notice refers to last semester, but I copy down the contact information anyway. It's worth a call to find out if the club meets during winter semester. I hope it does.

There's no doubt that I'm approaching the correct meeting room. Electrified conversations spill from a conference room, travel some distance down the hallway, and form a beacon that draws me into a meeting where people are sharing their enthusiasm for sailing. When I enter the room, I'm unsure about how to get involved in one of the conversations so I look around for a place to sit. Just when I've picked out a spot in the back of the room, someone taps my shoulder.

"Are you Valerie?"

"Yeah."

"Hi, I'm Kevin, the person you spoke with by phone. Welcome to our meeting."

Kevin, a husky man with thinning blonde hair, is about to introduce me to a few other club members when a woman at the front of the room tries to call the meeting to order.

"That's Carla." Kevin nods in the woman's direction. "She's this year's commodore and wants to begin the meeting, so let's take a seat."

"Commodore?"

"A sailing club's president is called a commodore."

Carla slaps her hand on the lectern, but few people notice. Kevin, raises his operatic voice and projects, "Okay folks, let's get the meeting started."

I take a seat next to Kevin who whispers, "I was last year's commodore and know how hard it is to get this group settled down. Valerie, let me know if you have any questions during the meeting, and I'll do my best to answer them."

"All right, everyone. I have something you'll want to hear." That announcement gets everyone's attention. "I, along with the club's board, nailed down two weekends in April for our spring work parties. We'll do prep work on Saturday, April 12. Then, we'll get the dock in and the boats ready the weekend of April 26 and 27." Although the dates are several months away, cheers and applause pour from the members.

When the excited chatter wanes, Carla completes some routine club business before introducing a guest speaker from the U.S. Power Squadron who goes over the basics of reading a navigation chart. The chart, or map, he displays on the screen shows a portion of Lake Erie. The speaker points out notations about water depth, hazards, and channel markers as well as other aids to navigation. His discussion of plotting coordinates is advanced so Kevin promises to help me understand how to read a chart's latitude and longitude over lunch next week. After the meeting adjourns, the club's secretary gives me a membership application and a schedule of topics to be covered during the club's off-season, indoor meetings.

Over the winter semester, I attend all the boat school lectures and read books about sailing. I'm determined to learn as much as I can before we gather at the clubhouse to ready the dock and boats in April. Kevin and I meet on campus at least once a week for a late lunch. He shows me how to tie sailing knots and answers questions I have based on my reading. I begin learning the parts of a sailboat, how to recognize the various navigational aids, and how to chart a course.

I get caught up in the currents that make Kevin's and the club members' lives flow. The palpable excitement exuded by the sailing club members at each meeting and by Kevin as he shares what he knows keeps me afloat as I struggle with what to do about work after my boss retires. I know I'm not totally on course away from the urge to do drugs, but I sense that I'm heading in a positive direction. I am navigating life without the benefit of a compass, but I have a strong conviction that I'm on the right point of sail. I hope that following that intuition is based on good faith and not on foolishness.

By the time the club meets at the boathouse in April, I'm confident about performing the tasks required. The winter boat lectures, my study of sailing books, and Kevin's tutoring did a great job of preparing me to work with the experienced members and handle the shore work. We move the boats out of the boathouse, dismantle the storage racks that held the boats during the off season, and move sections of the floating dock to the shore. Club members with wetsuits enter the chilly water while I assist others who line up dock pieces. Sometimes members stand at the edge of the lake hungering for enough warmth to make the remaining patches of ice go away so they can begin to sail. They are impatient, but they have no doubt that the icy, dark winter will pass into good sailing weather.

"Wow," I squeal as the wind grabs the sail and plunges our JY-15 sailboat through icy spray. Kevin commands the boat using the mainsail and tiller while I assist by handling the jib sail. He shows me how to counterbalance the tug of a sail filled with wind and keep our boat from capsizing.

"We need to use our weight on small boats," he explains, "since they do not have ballast for stability. Our weight keeps them upright especially in strong winds."

We sit on the gunwale, which is the top edge of the cockpit, anchor our feet beneath a strap secured to the bottom of the boat, and lean back to put much of our body weight over the water when strong puffs of wind fill the sail and threaten to capsize us. The sail-wind-weight trinity makes the boat feel alive as it cuts through the water. Handling the line to the jib energizes me as I learn to counterbalance my body against the wind. Traveling across the water and cutting through white-capped waves while holding the wind in the sail is intoxicating. For the first time in my life, I am connected to the elements around me in a way that lights up my eyes, enlivens my soul, and makes me crave more.

"This is amazing," I yell after a large, icy whitecap douses spray up over the bow and onto me and Kevin. I'm glad Kevin advised me to get a neoprene suit which keeps my body heat inside the wetsuit after cold waves wash over me. We're having a thrilling sail, and I see smiles on the other club members as the brisk wind hurtles our boats past each other.

Since our boats do not have lights, we stop sailing when the sun goes down. After returning the boats to shore, storing the sails, and changing into dry clothes, we gather near the clubhouse fire pit. I can see in our exhilarated eyes and in the high color in our faces that we carry life-giving, internal fires.

By June's summer solstice, I've learned how to ride the edge of capsize on a Laser sailboat. The Laser, designed to be single-handed, is a nimble boat that is popular with novice as well as professional sailors. If you're good enough, you can even qualify for Olympic sailing events on this type of boat. The small vessel remains upright in strong wind only if the sailor properly manages the single sail while counterbalancing the boat with his or her body weight.

I thrive on taking the Laser into challenging winds and learn to tack or turn the boat before crashing into shore or some other obstacle. As the boat changes direction, the boom whips from one side of the boat to the other while I duck underneath. It's a tricky maneuver because it requires a quick succession of movements. I free my feet from the strap at the bottom of the boat, move from one gunwale to the opposite side, re-anchor my feet under the strap, readjust the mainsail, and move the correct amount of weight outside the boat to offset the pull of the wind.

Over the summer, my growing skill at holding the wind in the sail and feeling the pulse of the waves on the hull gives me a more confident grip on myself and my life. I feel more assured, and that keeps worries about my future in check. I recently spent a couple of weeks in the accounting department where I'll be transferred in a couple days to begin fulltime work. I've also cut my visits to Dr. Z from two afternoons to one evening a week. I remain uncertain about whether I'll return to school.

In early August, Michael and his father visit the sailing club as my guests. They leave for Florida in a few days to live with Joe's sister, Michael's real aunty.

Michael doesn't want to sail, and I don't blame him. The day is breezy and a bit chilly so we take a walk along the club's beach, which is more dirt and pebbles than sand. We watch a few hearty club members as they sail and wind surf, and I let Michael climb aboard one of the onshore boats. It's too chilly to stay long at the edge of the lake so we return to the clubhouse where Joe sits with Kevin on a bench protected from the wind. Michael begins tugging at Joe's sleeve.

"All right, Michael," Joe concedes as he gives me a wink. He and Michael walk up the hill to the parking area and return with a gift. Joe tells me, "Michael picked this out for you."

The package is wrapped roughly by a child's hands and decorated with Crayola-drawings of flowers and butterflies.

"Open it. Open it," Michael encourages.

"Geez, Michael, it's so good-looking a package, it's a shame to open it, but I will if you want me to."

He jumps up and down clapping his hands and nodding his head. "Keep baby birds safe," Michael exclaims.

Inside the package is a kit for building a birdhouse, and it cuts through my denial over his moving away.

"Michael, it's a wonderful gift for me and the birds." It's hard for me to say more because Michael's thoughtfulness and generosity bring on tears that I fight to keep from spilling down my cheeks.

I give Michael a hug, and let him go before I start crying. He's excited about moving to Florida, and I don't want him to see how much it pains me that he's going away. I'm glad when Joe says they need to leave the club because I'm having difficulty choking back my sadness. I keep control over myself long enough for our good-byes to be happy ones so that Michael is free to go and take on his new life. I don't want any sadness to hold him back. He will always be a part of who I am, and I suspect that I will always be a part of who he becomes as he grows.

That evening, Kevin and I sit on the end of the floating dock watching the sun go down and the clouds become marked with a range of orange and red hues. Geese in V-formation honk to each other as they pass overhead. It's the end of the weekend, and I put off thinking about returning for another boring week at work. I've been employed fulltime for a month now at a job that is very repetitive with a salary that is much reduced from what I earned as an administrative assistant.

Kevin asks, "Have you decided what you're going to do in September? Will you continue working fulltime?"

"Boy, I hate thinking about it. I could continue working and take a night course or two. If I quit to go to school fulltime, I'm not sure what major to declare."

"I'll miss seeing you on campus if you don't come back for day classes. You know, I sometimes think about going to a different school."

"Really? Where would you go?"

"There's a school in North Carolina that teaches boat maintenance, anything from fiberglass repair to marine electrical systems to diesel engine mechanics. It's a marine trade school rather than a college or university."

"It sounds like a terrific career for a boater."

"Yeah, and the school is located near a protected body of water near the ocean. It's warmer there, and you can sail all year."

"Will you apply?"

Kevin sighs. "I doubt it. I'm basically a homebody. I grew up here and would miss my family and friends if I went out of state."

At home that night, I think about Michael and his father moving to Florida where there's a new life for Michael and a new job for Joe. Then, I think about Kevin's reluctance to move away from the safety he feels in the area where he grew up. I'm torn between staying put as Kevin does and moving into uncharted areas of my life like Michael and Joe are doing. Tomorrow, I begin another stifling workweek. I need to do something because I won't survive long in a mind-numbing clerical position with no hope of advancement. Since I began sailing, I rarely experience the urge to do drugs and drink less than I did before, but I wonder what will happen when the sailing season ends.

I open my medicine cabinet to look at the pills I haven't been able to discard. I raise my middle finger to the universe and its feckless whims and think, *I'm not ready to quit work for the unknown. Why am I forced to make a decision when I'm only now beginning to feel good about myself?* I'm frustrated and on the verge of using the pills Bill gave me. I pour enough alcohol into a cup to drown the urge to take the pills and know that if I drink it all, I'll regret it in the morning, but decisions must be made. After drinking the whiskey, I make a series of quick decisions:

I decide to give two weeks' notice in the morning.

I decide to stop seeing Dr. Z because my benefits will end when I leave my job.

I decide against returning to college for the fall 2003 term.

I decide to stop all drugs, including alcohol.

I've been navigating by faith ever since I discovered sailing and have made my decisions on an inner conviction that I am traveling in the right direction. I did not create and consult a list of pros and cons or make a deep analysis of what should or should not be done. Instead, I trust that the decisions I made will set me on a correct course. The pull I feel in that single direction is as strong as the magnetic tug on a compass needle. I plan to travel with the faith that my new course won't lead me into confused seas. I trust in my need to sail out to a different horizon even if that means I chance falling off some unforeseen edge.

Epilogue - Summer Solstice 2008

I will not follow where the path may lead,
but I will go where there is no path,
and I will leave a trail.
Muriel Strode, "Wind-Wafted Wild Flowers," 1903

"MORNIN' CAP'N," MARTY SAYS as he hands me a mug of coffee from the companionway steps.

When I take the warm mug into my chilled hands, I'm reminded of the time I drank hot chocolate with Kurt after we watched the sun's fire pierce through icicles on our first date. I'm onboard my Pacific Seacraft, a sailboat similar to Skipper's, and completing an overnight passage from Milwaukee, Wisconsin, to Muskegon, Michigan. All night long, winds pushed spray over the bow and the journey was rough, but the wind on Lake Michigan has settled down a few hours before dawn. I take in the smell of the rich, dark java and relax.

Marty, a Desert Storm veteran who often crews for me, remains below and studies the Lake Michigan chart. I call out, "How far are we from shore?"

"About eight miles."

"Good. We should see nav lights soon."

I take time to study the stars before picking up the binoculars and looking for signs of shore.

"How's Bean doing after that rocky ride?"

"She's fine, nestled in her usual spot." Bean isn't fond of sailing and hunkers behind a pillow at the front of the salon's main berth.

It's a crisp, clear night. No moon blots out a view of the Milky Way. The constellation Perseus sparkles over the bow, and a starry web of twinkling dots is spread over Lake Michigan skies acting as ancient beacons. I'm awake on nights like this not because of nightmares, insomnia or amphetamines but because life is too keen, too wonderful, to be asleep. While sailing at night, I'm guided by the stars as much as I navigate within the spidery network of longitude and latitude coordinates on a marine map. The onboard need to trust in yourself, your crew, and the world is shared by mariners, ancient and contemporary. No one goes far from shore without knowing the risks and gauging their ability to deal with them.

Marty enters the cockpit and points to an area off the starboard bow. I take up the binoculars and see a red light that's on for three seconds and then dark for three seconds. The pattern repeats. We are on course for Muskegon Lake.

As we get closer to land, we see recreational fishing boats heading out in the predawn hours and hear the early-morning chatter of friends on the VHF marine radio as it scans channels. It has been a long night, and we look forward to docking and getting some breakfast. Tomorrow, we will be joined by a couple of veterans from the Afghanistan conflict. I will ask them, as I ask all veterans I meet, if they have talked with someone who might be Kurt.

When I quit my job and left college, I enrolled in the marine technical school that Kevin mentioned when we talked at the sailing club after Michael's visit. I specialized in marine diesel engines and travel to customers in need of service. I also earned a captain's license and volunteer my time and my sailboat at a veterans' organization where I teach wounded veterans how to sail.

As I travel, I draw on the Appalachian Trail tradition of "trail magic" whereby nonhikers leave useful items at trailheads for hikers. In honor of that convention, I leave boxes of nonperishable food, warm clothes, and rain ponchos wherever I see evidence of homeless veterans. Maybe Kurt benefits from some of the items left on that trail.

Skipper searches for Kurt in his own way, and we are certain that Kurt will eventually reach out to one of us for help. A couple of times each year, I visit him and Barbara and sail with Skipper on San Diego Bay.

We talk about marine issues because we have an unstated agreement that we will only talk about Kurt when he resurfaces in our lives. Sometimes, we find a quiet place to anchor overnight and enjoy a sunset, the night-time sky, and the morning symphony of squawking seagulls.

Mom was never able to step far beyond her narrow take on life. She still retreats into her monologues during our talks and uses many trite phrases to circumvent establishing a deeper connection with me. It's okay. I know I how difficult it is to change and do not require it of her.

As my sailboat approaches the Muskegon lighthouse and the rising sun, I stand balanced with one foot on each side of the sailboat's centerline. My right hand holds the tiller behind me, and my other hand rests on the cabin top in front of me. I'm in easy command of my vessel but scan the horizon knowing that an approaching storm could make the journey difficult, even dangerous. Today's probability for a storm is low, but it pays to keep an eye on the clouds in the sky, watch the tell-tale signs of wind shifts on water, and know the location of harbors of refuge.

About the Author

The author earned a Ph.D. in Sociology from Indiana University-Bloomington. Her published research involves graffiti, gangs, policing, and restorative justice. She lives in Calabash, North Carolina.